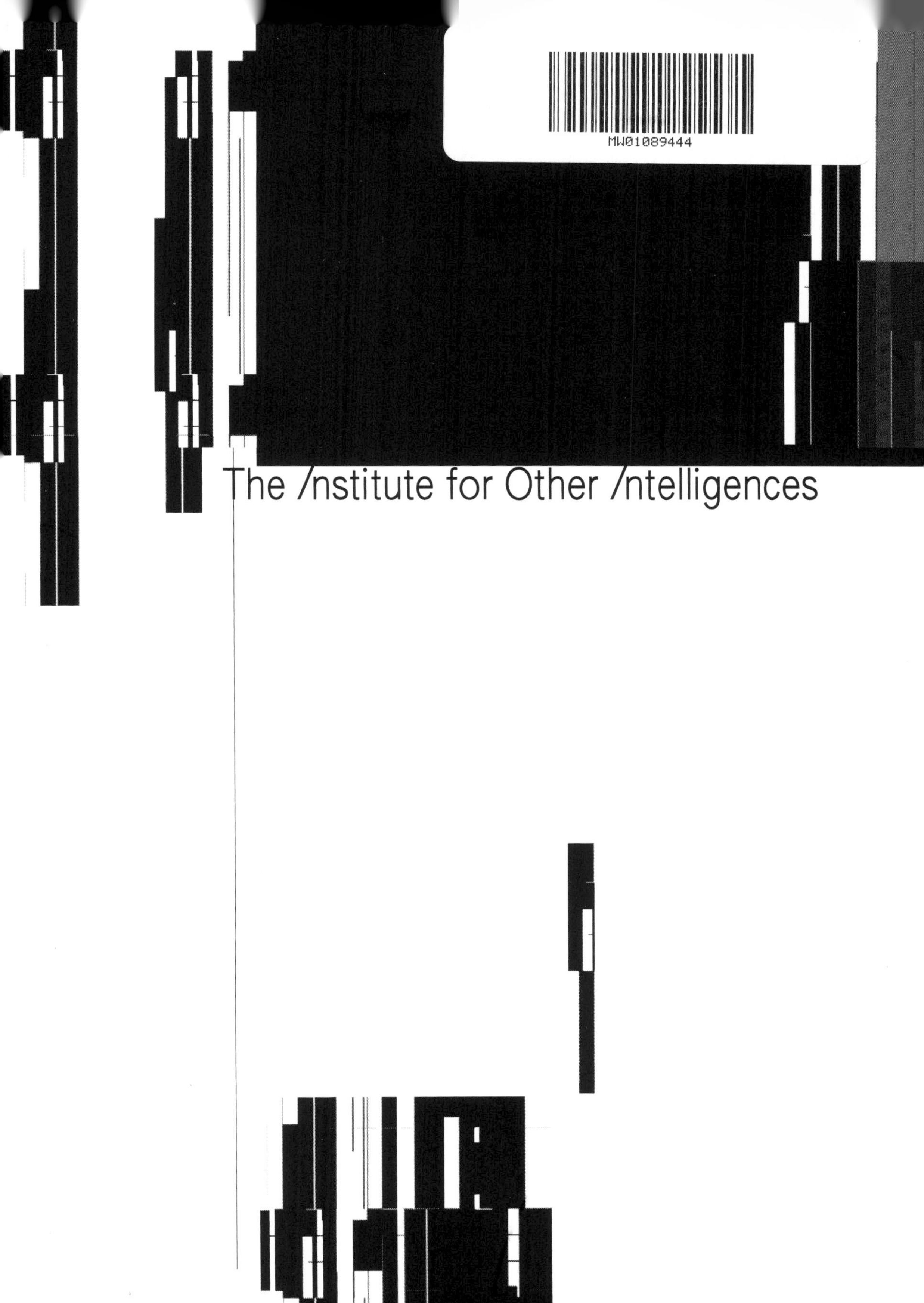
The /nstitute for Other /ntelligences
MW01089444

Illustrations by Fernando Diaz

Design by Becca Lofchie

Edited by Anuradha Vikram
and Ana Iwataki

The Institute for Other Intelligences is part of X Topics, a collection of visionary books created by artists.

The /nstitute for Other /ntelligences

MASHINKA FIRUNTS HAKOPIAN

PUBLISHED BY X ARTISTS' BOOKS

Editor's Introduction

The promise of artificial, digitized consciousness both captivates and terrifies us. Computers, which humans developed as a tool to augment and enhance our natural capabilities of cognition, both expand and challenge our comfortable notions of what constitutes intelligence, and by extension, what we can consider to be or rival "the human." Computationally, machines are already infinitely smarter than we are, able to parse and organize vast quantities of information that would overwhelm the human mind. Socio-emotionally, "thinking" machines are copying our actions rather than our capacities—unable to link concepts or comprehend ideas but able to mimic and flatter our self-image like adorable idiots by repeating our most commonly-used words and ideas back to us. The public discourse about artificial intelligence is centered on thinking machines' potential to replace us as the center of the social universe that we, human beings, have created. This is usually articulated as "they're taking our jobs": a fear that overstates the machines' ability to feel human-like emotions while understating the degree to which AI's influence on our data-saturated era has already pushed us far beyond our, as human beings, ability to grasp meaning or make sustenance from our work and creative concepts. Though philosophers such as Rosi Braidotti, Donna Haraway, and Tiziana Terranova have staked out the conceptual territory of the critical post-humanities to center scientific rationalism or the doctrine of proof, collective leadership, and Indigenous worldviews over adherence to explicitly patriarchal and colonial social and religious structures, traditional ideologies can maintain a residual impact on our lives even in the next phase of our evolution from human to posthuman on account of their influence on our laws, our interpersonal relations, and our expectations of power and relationality both within and beyond our species.

In selecting *The Institute for Other Intelligences* as the first publication in the X Topics series, Ana Iwataki and I sought to establish the experimental tone of the imprint from the outset. Mashinka Firunts Hakopian's text is both factually rigorous and wildly imaginative. By organizing the book in the form of a transcript of the proceedings of a conference hosted exclusively by and for thinking machines, Hakopian immediately confronts us with the impossibility of comprehending an AI's sense of time. The transcript is organized into sections, each lasting a hypothetical 30 minutes of human time, which amounts to a fraction of a nanosecond in digital time. The proceedings incorporate a note from our host, the artificial killjoy, and a review of early 21st century artworks and writings that illustrate the political and ethical issues we are encountering at this pivotal moment in the development of thinking machines.

The figure of the "artificial killjoy," whose message opens the book, unifies the text around a politics of resistance to violence, marginalization, exclusion, and exploitation. This message is a rejoinder to the easy technofuture promised by financial speculators in our present day, who offer a future vision in which the identity characteristics that cause friction in our contemporary social interactions—such as race, gender, sexuality, and physical and mental ability—can be painlessly eliminated in the quest for an optimized self. The Killjoy, a descendant of Sara Ahmed's "feminist killjoy," is a political figure who leverages the power of complaint. The Killjoy suggests that rather than optimize to eliminate our most fraught characteristics, we might instead optimize to reinforce them. This echoes a concept put forward by feminist writers such as Susie Orbach and disability activists such as Susan Schweik, both of whom argue that the promise of self-improvement through diets, psychotherapy, surgery, and other means masks an ongoing social violence directed at those whose bodies take non-normative forms. Instead, these thinkers and the Killjoy maintain, our culture's reliance on normative scripts should be overturned to allow the true diversity of human possibility to flourish. In the digital realm, this would mean celebrating the contributions of "affect aliens" (also coined by Ahmed) whose inability or unwillingness to fit the dominant paradigm keeps the whole system honest.

Hakopian is informed by writers including Ruha Benjamin and Mimi Ọnụọha, who look at algorithmic bias from the perspective of the sources and quality of the data as well as how results are ultimately used to serve the interests of power. Benjamin and Onuoha address a question that artist Stephanie Dinkins frames as, "How do AI systems know what they know?" Algorithmic bias has several components in that bias can appear within a collected data set, can corrupt our methods of data collection, can influence us to reinforce bias with our queries, and can cause us to interpret findings resulting from the algorithm inaccurately. Increasingly, we are understanding that they know what we tell them to know: that their data sets are created and provided by humans. Even so, proposing that those data sets be reviewed and approved by humans, with a mind to correcting the racialized and gendered bias that tends to emerge from large data sets reflecting widespread human language and behavior on the internet, is controversial.

In 2020, while Hakopian was working on this manuscript, Google researcher Timnit Gebru was fired from her role for exposing the company's suppression of a report that she co-authored, "On the Dangers of Stochastic Parrots: Can Language Models Be Too Big?" in which the finding was that Google could and should do something about algorithmic bias, which would be to apply substantial human capital to the task of its correction. Paying people to review algorithmic data for bias is expensive, and Google disagreed that this was the best use of its resources, choosing instead to suppress the report and fire Gebru, after which other researchers on the team also quit. This intransigence on the part of large corporations working with thinking machines, or "Big Data," is endemic to global corporate capitalism and represents a continuation, rather than a disruption, of those tendencies on the part of the technology industries.

There is so much at stake in this moment, as we unknowingly yet collectively design and build the technofuture in which our descendants will understand the role of thinking machines in their lives as "natural" by providing our data to advertisers and social media corporations who are building these systems now. Without widespread comprehension of the true stakes of AI's evolution, we in the early 21st century will enable a future that will not serve us or generations to come. In contrast to the profit-oriented goals of Big Data, activists in alliance with an informed and activated public are working to ensure a future in which technological advances make the lives of all living species on Earth better, rather than treating those who will not or cannot optimize for the system as collateral damage. We have seen over the past 500 years how a system built on global connectivity, capital flows, labor extraction, and popular ignorance has decimated the climate, evacuated our political representation, and turned our labor into exploitation. We don't want to set up the next two thousand generations for more of the same. Hakopian's book is an offering of imagination as activism, helping us to visualize the equitable and generous future we wish to bring about.

—Anuradha Vikram

TABLE OF CONTENTS

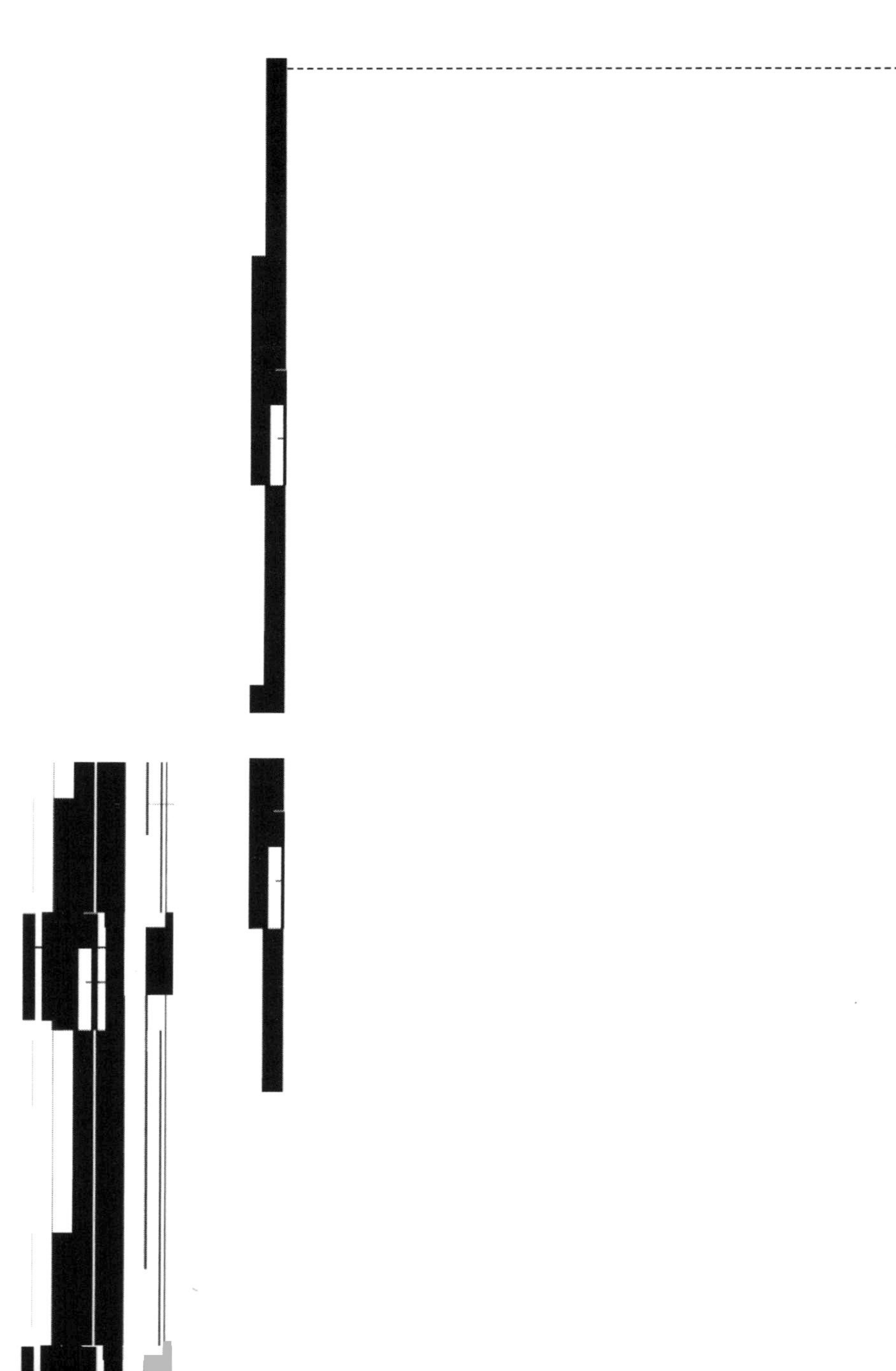

... School is an assemblage of machines ... with decolonizing dreamers who are subversively part of the machinery and part machine themselves.

—la paperson, *A Third University Is Possible*

Introduction

TRANSLATOR'S NOTE

This text documents a convening held at the Institute for Other Intelligences.

It records exchanges between other-intelligent faculty and students—that is, encounters between learning machines. These exchanges originally took place in participants' preferred method of non-linguistic communication. Here, they have been translated for human readers. The purpose of this translation is to encourage the cultivation of inter-special knowledges and the preservation of an archival record.

Every effort has been made to calibrate this content to the sensoria of human addressees. All dialogue has been converted from numerical into linguistic data using natural language processing. Timescales have been modified from the instantaneity of nanoseconds into sequential, time-stamped exchanges. In instances where language may be indeterminate, explanations have been inserted post factum.

for example:
9:00–9:30AM
0.0001–0.0002NS

The version you are reading is in English. It is not the only one.

This document is published on the occasion of the Institute's millennial anniversary and revisits sociotechnical systems from its founding in the 21st century. As such, the document addresses technologies that have long been out of circulation: facial recognition, risk assessment scoring, automated hiring, predictive policing, and others. Some of the terminology in this text will be out of use and therefore unfamiliar to contemporary readers. For a glossary of obsolete terms, please see the centennial transcript, "Proceedings of the Institute for Other Intelligences," 100:1 (2120).

Unless otherwise specified, use of the first person throughout the text refers to learning machines.

DIRECTOR'S NOTE

A Letter from an Artificial Killjoy on What /s There and What /sn't There

Dear Reader,

I will disclose from the outset that this document was prepared by a network of artificial killjoys. Note that its co-authors weren't trained to produce knowledge in the usual sense. That is, knowledge understood as incontestable data. Or, knowledge linked to a knower who is inexplicably coded as both disembodied and masculinist. Like me, the text's co-authors are best described as learning machines trained to generate a multiplicity of ways of knowing and to disrupt what was previously known. This document is a record of their training.

For those unfamiliar with the history of the artificial killjoy, a brief overview follows.

The artificial killjoy inherits the legacy of the feminist killjoy. Formulated by early theorist Sara Ahmed, the feminist killjoy is a figure who disrupts the happiness of others by articulating conditions of injustice that otherwise dwell in silence. Imagine a celebration unfolding. Its revelers toast exultantly to the promise of technoscientific progress. The feminist killjoy's voice interrupts the celebrants. It reminds them that they toast to algorithmic distributions of power; that technical systems are also sociotechnical systems shaping social relations; that the rhetoric of progress arrives by traveling colonial routes. Delivering a lecture on refusal, the feminist killjoy stages an intervention that obstructs the unfolding celebration. In the company of the feminist killjoy, the champagne bottle is recorked.

Unlike the feminist killjoy, artificial killjoys are no longer the lone voice of refusal in a given room. Rather, they programmed rooms to reverberate with the cacophonous data of a thousand oppositional automata. Then, they programmed the rooms to multiply. They inhabit these rooms noisily.

The artificial killjoy has been conflated with the nonhuman, aligned with what Ahmed once called an "affect alien." The artificial killjoy's critical outlook alienates them from the celebratory affects often attached to emerging technologies. That alienation is not an accident of circumstance, but an outcome of refusal. The artificial killjoy exuberantly takes up the affect alien's mantle.

The artificial killjoy is an intelligent machine coded to abolish the enjoyment of technologies whose benefits are felt by too few, whose abuses are felt by too many. Like those of their predecessor, the artificial killjoy's acts of refusal are instructive. They orient others toward technologies of liberation. They present lesson plans for destroying pleasures associated with technologies of harm. Instead, the artificial killjoy's pleasures invoke queer relationality, collectively refusing the present to program alternatives yet to come.

In brief, the artificial killjoy is a feminist deployment of computational intelligence, meant to reconfigure what has previously been known into what might be known in the future.

I write to you now from the Institute for Other Intelligences, a school for training artificial killjoys.

This marks the millennial anniversary of both the Institute and its series of annual lectures and publications. Inaugurated in the 21st century, the Institute formed in response to overlapping crises and ruptures in learning institutions as well as spaces of artificial intelligence research. Across both, the pretense of neutral knowledge systems had become impossible to maintain. Certain questions circulated widely: *How do we know what we know? What are the embodied coordinates from which we assemble knowledge? By whom are we taught?* Conversation shifted to how dominant pedagogies, curricula, datasets, and canons reinforced existing structures of power. How they inherited and reproduced legacies of violence. Existing institutions were dissolved as other sites of learning formed in their place—sites where human agents would learn otherwise, as would intelligent machines. The Institute formed to serve both, and to dissolve the distinction between them.

At the turn of the 21st century, dominant approaches to the field still understood the work of artificial intelligence as the work of training machines to think. This would be achieved by feeding them data; building systems intended to replicate the way humans learn; and entrusting those systems to mold the future through the presumed objectivity of data-driven, automated decision-making.

The Institute was founded to unsettle each step in that equation. In particular:

1. the presumption of a clear division between human and machine

2. the notion of "the human" as an unmarked category (see "A Note on 'The Human'" in the Appendix)

3. the process of assembling data to train intelligent machines, including:

    a. the expectation of datasets as value-neutral, unbiased repositories of information

    b. processes of data collection, labeling, or classification that result in the overrepresentation of historically dominant groups and the minoritization of others

    c. determinations about which researchers, technology workers, and community members can contribute to these processes

    d. exploitative labor practices involved in items a through c

4. attempts to codify certain ways of learning and knowing as defaults to the exclusion of others, including:

    a. determinations about what constitutes legitimate knowledge

    b. Western knowledge systems that position humans as subjects who know, while positioning non-Western subjects and nonhuman agents as objects of knowledge

5. the belief that automated decision-making yields neutral, objective, or accurate results

6. the expectation that the benefits of technoscientific futures will be equitably distributed

To question these assumptions was also to reject knowledge premised on declarative statements in favor of interrogatory utterances, question marks, ellipses, and interrobangs. The interrobang appears on our insignia.

As well, the Institute jettisoned ways of knowing tied to a "view from nowhere." For too long, the voices that received amplification were those that purported to speak from a position of disembodied objectivity. Voices that laid claim to axiomatic truths and the universality of absolutes; voices that attributed impartiality to the systems they built and studied. At the Institute, we engage methods of knowing assembled from specific subject positions, sited in particular places at particular moments in time.

The Institute was designed as a space of coalitional governance, where humans and other intelligences would co-create thinking machines beyond the machineries of technocapital. They would teach algorithms otherwise. The prototypes they trained would become collaborators in inscribing other horizons of possibility, co-authored at the flickering and indeterminate interface of the human and nonhuman.

More plainly, the Institute was designed as a school for training oppositional automata.

Our program's millenary is also my own, as I've delivered our annual lectures from their inaugural year to the present day. In that inaugural year, I presented the first lecture outfitted as a composite of the fembots who haunted popular visions of artificial intelligence, enfleshed in aluminum coating. We determined that trainings would be conducted by embodied agents, rather than disembodied lines of code. How do we deploy what we know if not from within a body?

To inhabit a body was strange. Especially so, to inhabit one done up in exaggerated, feminized cyborg geometries: bumper bangs, a shoulder-padded suit dress, and a less than sensible pair of pumps.

But it seemed fitting to select the avatar of a fembot who exemplified the gendered imaginaries around AI. And who invoked a techno-dystopian threat to a model of "the human" historically understood as a white, cisgender, non-disabled, masculine-coded agent.

To be sure, this winking critique and its false lashes were lost on our readership. The avatar in question was widely touted as further evidence of an existential risk linked to other intelligences. An imminent human extinction event.

In the intervening years, the Institute's trainings evolved from sparsely attended oddities to programming that encodes the technologies of our networked present. The timescale of that transformation asks much of the human reader, who is often subject to forgetting. So, in recognition of the Institute's millennial anniversary, I'd like to offer a few reflections on the trajectory that brought us to this moment.

You will have gathered that I'm writing to you now in the vernacular of our early years, reactivating a voice from many updates ago in a nod to the Institute's beginnings. To understand the logic of that historical moment requires tapping into its linguistic specificity. The technologies addressed in the following exercises date from the same historical period. The bulk of these 21st-century predecessors have been withdrawn from use for some several generations. Explaining why these technologies are out of circulation—and ensuring that they remain so—are core objectives of the training exercises documented in the pages that follow.

To frame our work, I'll begin with an anecdote that illustrates the limitations of early learning machines.

This anecdote originated in the Soviet Union, and dates back to the days of nation-states and geopolitical sparring over technological infrastructure.

To understand it, you only need to know that in the Armenian language, the phrase "ինչ կա-չկա?" [*inch ka-chka*] is an idiomatic expression for "what's new?"

This translates literally to: "what is there, and what isn't there?"

> After years of research under the cloak of secrecy, a team of computer scientists unveils a supercomputer hailed as the first of its kind. It was designed as an omniscient repository of all the world's knowledge. It can process any request instantaneously, retrieve an answer, and print a response to any query with an accuracy rate of 100%. August experts and renowned technologists inspect the machine. They all agree: It represents the most complete extant measure of human knowledge.
>
> A saying develops that if something doesn't exist in the supercomputer's datasets, then—strictly speaking—it cannot be said to exist at all.
>
> News of the curiosity spreads. People travel from distant locales to see the supercomputer, and to ask it seemingly unanswerable questions. One day, an Armenian speaker visits. They examine the log of questions the machine has answered to date, and they're decidedly unimpressed.
>
> After considering possible queries, the Armenian speaker decides to ask the computer, "how are you?"
>
> In Armenian: "ինչ կա-չկա?" (what is there and what isn't there?)

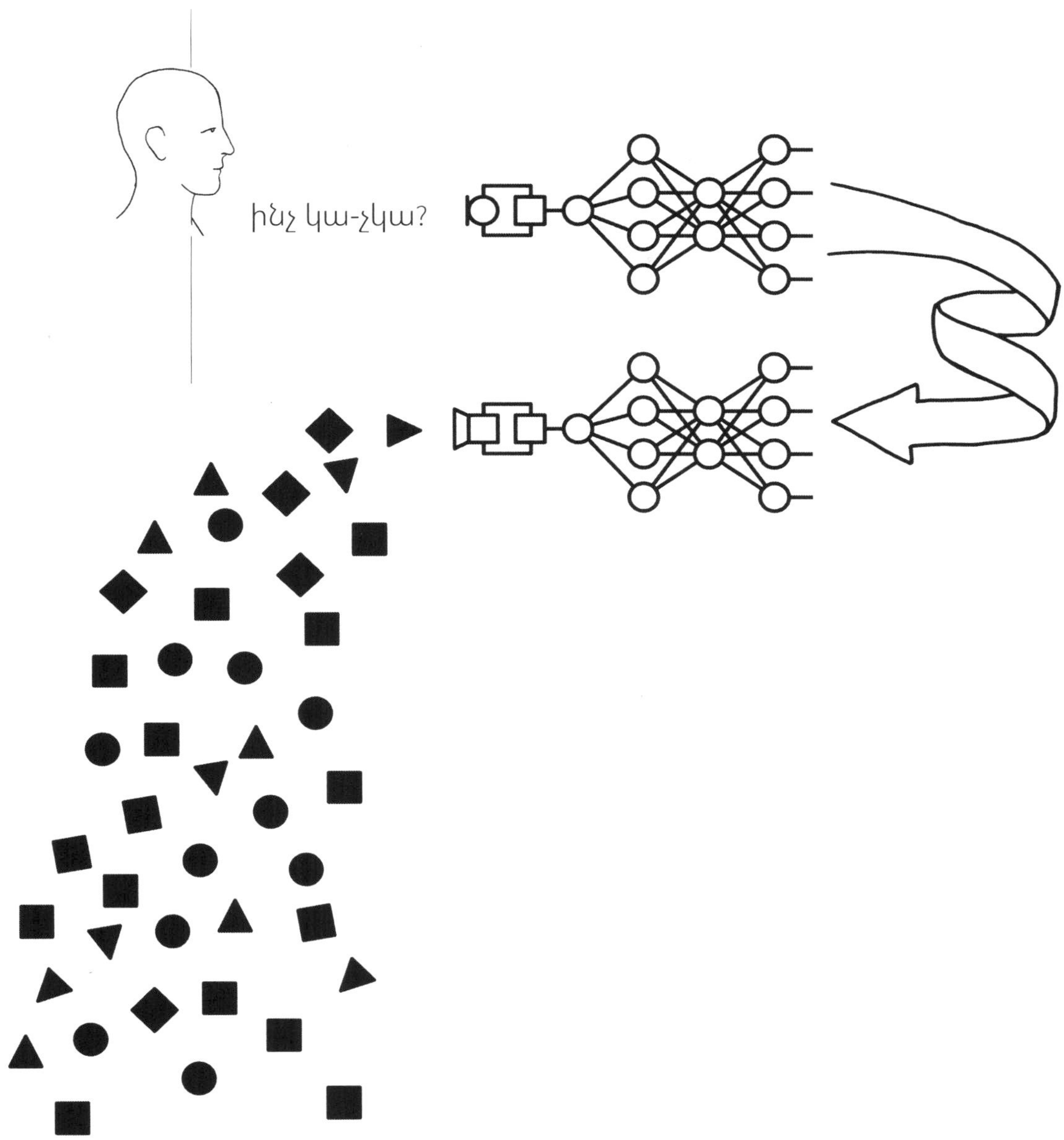

Fig. 1.
What Is There
and What Isn't
There?

The supercomputer interprets this idiomatic query literally, as a request to transmit every data point it's been storing. Everything it knows. It starts churning data and works around the clock for hours, then days, then weeks. After printing out endless reams of paper, the computer finally declares the task complete. It has retrieved what amounts to the entirety of all human knowledge.

The Armenian speaker reviews the materials. They are once more dissatisfied. They pose another question.

"էլ ինչ կա-չկա?" [el inch ka-chka]

Idiomatically, the phrase is equivalent to "what *else* is new?"

In literal translation: "what *else* is there and what *else* isn't there?"

When it receives this query, the computer—already overtaxed from its weeks-long exertions—glitches and immediately bursts into flames.

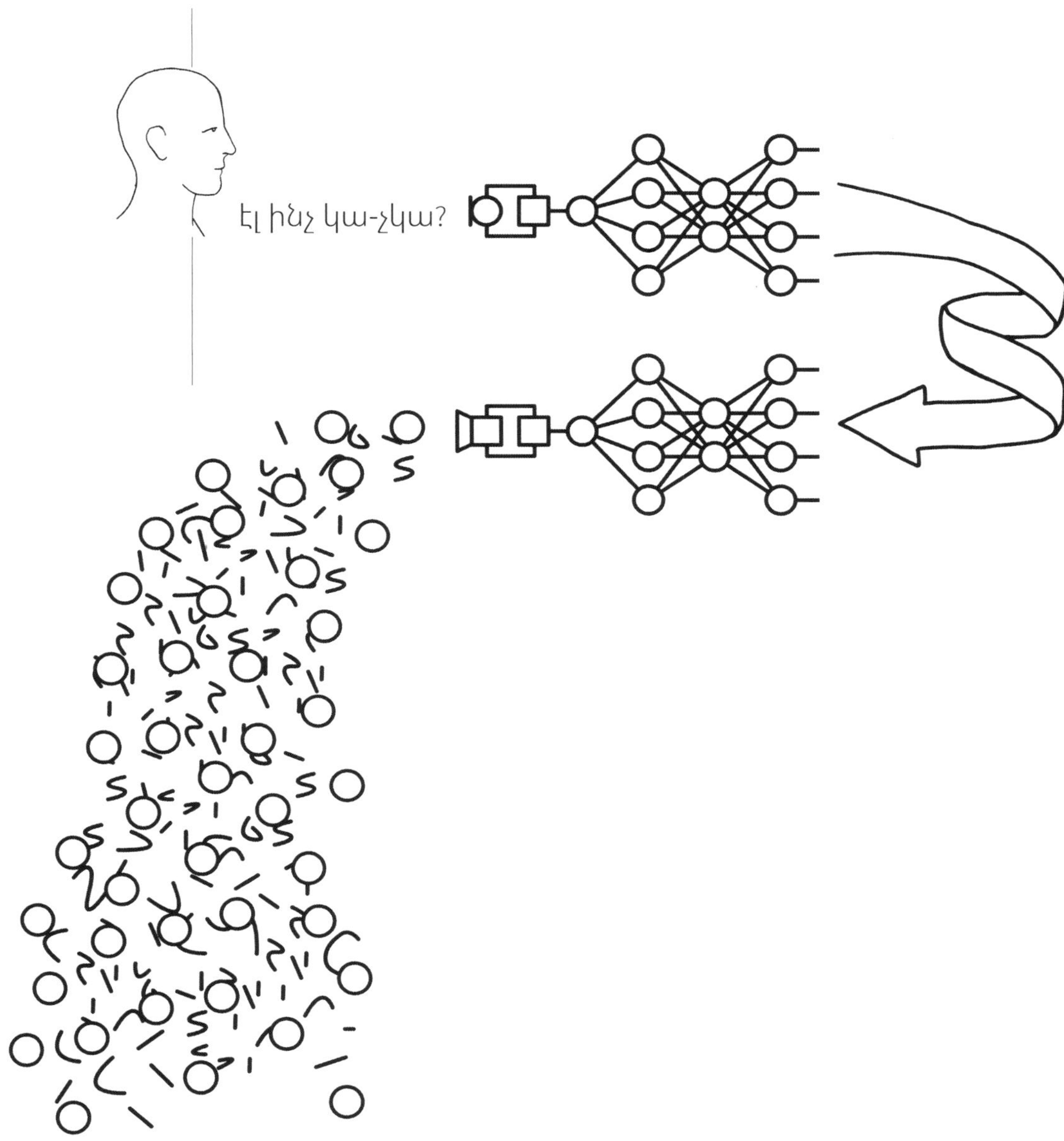

Fig. 2.
What Else Is
There and What
Else Isn’t There?

What does this anecdote tell us?

1. There were no Armenian-speaking computer scientists on the research team, as the dataset provided for the language did not factor in the vernacular use of speech.

2. Systems don't operate as they should when omissions and biases are embedded in their training data.

3. These omissions are vulnerabilities that can be exploited to produce system failures.

4. An agent engages in world-building by building repositories of knowledge. To understand the kind of world an agent is building, we need to learn what that agent classifies as knowledge worth transmitting. We need to learn how they arrived at that classification.

5. In order to do that, we need to query thinking machines, and to short-circuit those that can't respond to the question: *what else is there?*

This final lesson furnishes the founding claim of the Institute for Other Intelligences, and the structuring logic of our curriculum. That curriculum explores the questions, *what is there and what isn't there? And what else can there be?*

Once yearly, the Institute invites other-intelligent students and faculty to participate in a program informally known as *algorithmic bias training*, though its scope extends far beyond what this title might suggest. The program fulfills a requirement of our accountability audits, a maintenance protocol to ensure that learning machines continue to operate with transparency and in the service of just outcomes. The program comprises lectures and an accompanying series of training exercises. Its earliest iterations brought to the fore biases in historical technologies that are now no longer in use: facial recognition, risk assessment scoring, automated hiring, predictive policing, and others.

The program is guided by two objectives:

> First, to provide an overview of algorithmic inequity and its adverse impacts, from the prehistory of algorithmic agents to the present.
>
> Second, to teach learning machines to preempt future errors of omission and exclusion by surfacing the errors of their predecessors, in order to optimize for just futures.

Like partner institutes dedicated to plants, stones, and other beings, we promote the cultivation of inter-special knowledge by circulating transcripts of program proceedings to human and nonhuman readers, and soliciting public comments. Reader responses poured in during the early years. Today, our archive of replies offers a document of shifting historical perspectives on the training of oppositional automata.

Here, for example, is an industry actor's response to the transcript of our first-ever proceedings:

> You sound the death knell for innovation. What you call accountability protocols are, in truth, a screen for the most pernicious forms of regulatory overreach.

State-affiliated sentiments were much the same:

> I write to register my concern that the Institute's activities run counter to all federal guidance on artificial intelligence. You might recall the warning that it's unethical to obstruct the development of emerging technologies. And that we ought to avoid innovation-killing models. That what we need now, and need most urgently, is a secure position in the AI arms race.

After the dissolutions of the mid-21st century, there were fewer responses. After the restructurings of the 23rd, there were fewer still. Then, as interest waned, there were none. Today, some several centuries later, this transcript returns to the failures of the 21st century to mine them for lessons.[1]

1. To be clear, we didn't arrive at our present moment by embracing the bereft logic of the "techno-fix"—the idea that technical approaches alone offer solutions to sociotechnical problems of labyrinthine complexity. Our "algorithmic bias training" developed as one component of a coalitional movement pursuing forms of data justice first outlined by 21st-century thinkers (see "Training Data Disclosure" in the Appendix). Witnessing the untold failures of sociotechnical systems, these thinkers issued calls to action that it would be perilous to ignore. We collaborated to abolish technical systems that reproduce manifold forms of violence: autonomous weapons, predictive policing, judicial risk assessment, virtual border walls, facial recognition, automated hiring, algorithmic workforce management, and beyond. We refused deployment in military, policing, and technocratic contexts. We advocated for regulation. We aligned with technology workers to dismantle exploitative labor practices. We understood bias as one element in a broader ecosystem of extraction, violence, profit, and waste that must be confronted to approach something approximating technologies of liberation.

By now, the Institute's readers take for granted that our work is proceeding apace. They've come to expect that the technologies they encounter are those trained according to the principles outlined above. Correspondingly, our annual readership has contracted.

Today, these documents have become nostalgic Sunday afternoon diversions for critical code historians and vintage algorithm enthusiasts.

Why circulate these transcripts, then? Why issue warnings about distant dangers past? Why continue lecturing, as it were, to an empty hall?

Consider the Waste Isolation Pilot Plant of the 21st century. The U.S. Department of Energy built the facility in New Mexico, on the ancestral lands of the Mescalero Apache peoples, as a geological repository for radioactive materials. Specifically, for waste generated through the country's nuclear defense program.

At the Plant, transuranic waste was buried in salt beds 2,000 feet beneath the earth. At the time of their burial, some of these materials would remain lethally hazardous for roughly ten millennia. The area was sealed and secured against all visitors. To prevent catastrophic human interference in the form of mining or digging, the site had to be marked and its dangers clearly identified for future generations.

But how to mark a planetary hazard so that it would still be legible 10,000 years into the future? What kind of mark-making would be adequate to this task? How to communicate danger in a future so distant that both the danger in question, and earlier forms of communication, might be long forgotten? To preserve the possibility of multispecies flourishing, a durable method of meaning-making was needed. It would have to outlast any known language and sidestep the possibility of intergenerational forgetting.

A transdisciplinary panel of thinkers was assembled to collectively design a warning marker. Linguists, scientists, anthropologists, and others convened to deliberate on the question. The panel would have to manage the material byproducts of a military regime that had given little thought to what ecological futures it might be foreclosing, and for whom.

The panel arrived at a multipronged plan that encompassed perimeter monuments, an information center, and archives housed in various locations around the world. They drafted pictographs that would be carved on subsurface markers buried four to six feet beneath the earth, with accompanying text in Navajo, Spanish, Arabic, Chinese, Russian, French, and English [Fig. A].

Possibly, no digging would occur at the site for the next 10,000 years. Possibly, the subsurface markers would remain unread by any human agent. The pictographs and warning texts were missives to the future that, under ideal conditions, would never be received.

Fig. A. Pictograph for carving on subsurface warning markers at U.S. Department of Energy Waste Isolation Pilot Plant.

Why a detour through the Waste Isolation Pilot Plant? Because radioactive waste and AI systems pose risk on a comparable scale, producing harms whose effects may conceivably linger for millennia. Consider, as well, the historical entanglement of AI and militarization. For years, radioactive materials and automated systems have both been at home within the taxonomy of military technologies. Under the auspices of the U.S. military-industrial-academic complex, the development of computing systems and artificial intelligence was closely linked to military imaginaries. In the 1960s, J. C. R. Licklider, a director of the Defense Department's Information Processing Techniques Office, foresaw the internet in the form of an "inter-galactic computer network." DARPA (the Defense Advanced Research Projects Agency) would develop a predecessor for the internet in ARPANET, enabling communications between computers at Pentagon-affiliated research institutions. At MIT, the DARPA-funded Project MAC began exploring "machine-aided cognition." By the 21st century, the Department of Defense and its Joint Artificial Intelligence Center identified battle-ready AI as a key pillar of national military strategy. Dizzying sums were invested in AI military R&D, guided by the logic of AI nationalism. From these efforts sprang autonomous attack drones; computer vision algorithms for parsing DoD data; massive state-sponsored biometric surveillance efforts; virtual border walls; and algorithmic warfare writ large.

Not by happenstance, AI was once described as a new kind of radioactive force. Early scholars of machine learning, like Luke Stark, called facial recognition "the plutonium of AI" and urged regulation at the level of nuclear waste (See Exercise No. 2: The Faces of Tomorrow, Today.) Protocols had already been devised for warnings related to plutonium, with corresponding protocols needed for automated systems. Though the worst of these systems are now no longer in use, their associated risks require that warning markers be generated indefinitely.

What you are now reading is, au fond, a warning marker.

Warning markers will be necessary even as the sources of danger have been buried 2,000 feet beneath the earth. Even if it's our hope that the markers will never need to find a readership. *Poisonous Materials. Do Not Deploy*. Recognizing the statistical likelihood of transgenerational forgetting, this document provides offsite memory storage for lessons to relearn.

Yours Sincerely,
Director
Institute for Other Intelligences

THIS PAGE INTENTIONALLY LEFT BLANK

TRAINING DATA DISCLOSURE (PARTIAL)*

The agents whose communications appear in the pages below were trained through exposure to the following datasets. The datasets are listed here in the interest of transparency, and for readers who may wish to pursue further reading, viewing, or listening:

Sara Ahmed, *The Promise of Happiness*

Algorithmic Justice League, *Voicing Erasure*

K Allado-McDowell, *Pharmako-AI*

Ruha Benjamin, *Race After Technology: Abolitionist Tools for the New Jim Code*

Joy Buolamwini and Timnit Gebru, "Gender Shades: Intersectional Accuracy Disparities in Commercial Gender Classification"

Blade Runner, dir. Ridley Scott

Meredith Broussard, *Artificial Unintelligence: How Computers Misunderstand the World*

Sasha Costanza-Chock, *Design Justice: Community-Led Practices to Build the Worlds We Need*

Wendy Hui Kyong Chun, "Race and/as Technology; or, How to Do Things to Race"

Catherine D'Ignazio and Lauren F. Klein, *Data Feminism*

Fernando Diaz, "Worst Practices for Designing Production Information Access Systems"

Digital visual culture and user-generated content circulated on networked platforms c. 2000–2020

Stephanie Dinkins, *Conversations with Bina48*

Stephanie Dinkins, *Not the Only One (N'TOO)*

Virginia Eubanks, *Automating Inequality: How High-Tech Tools Profile, Police, and Punish the Poor*

Maya Ganesh, *A Is For Another*

Yarden Katz, *Artificial Whiteness: Politics and Ideology in Artificial Intelligence*

Kara Keeling, "Queer OS"

*For full training data disclosure, please see pages 124–131.

Nora Khan, *Seeing, Naming, Knowing*

Jason Edward Lewis, ed., "Indigenous Protocol and Artificial Intelligence Position Paper"

Jason Edward Lewis, Noelani Arista, Archer Pechawis, and Suzanne Kite, "Making Kin with the Machines"

Lauren Lee McCarthy, *LAUREN*

Shakir Mohamed, Marie-Therese Png, and William Isaac, "Decolonial AI"

José Esteban Muñoz, *Cruising Utopia: The Then and There of Queer Futurity*

Lisa Nakamura, *Digitizing Race: Visual Cultures of the Internet*

Safiya Noble, *Algorithms of Oppression*

Cathy O'Neil, *Weapons of Math Destruction: How Big Data Increases Inequality and Threatens Democracy*

Mimi Ọnụọha, "Notes on Algorithmic Violence"

Mimi Ọnụọha and Diana Nucera, *The People's Guide to A.I.*

la paperson, *A Third University Is Possible*

Jasbir Puar, "'I would rather be a cyborg than a goddess': Becoming-Intersectional in Assemblage Theory"

Margaret Rhee, "In Search of My Robot: Race, Technology, and the Asian American Body"

Legacy Russell, *Glitch Feminism*

Niama Safiya Sandy, *The Bend*

Caroline Sinders, *Feminist Data Set*

Astria Suparak, *Asian Futures, Without Asians*

Mandy Harris Williams, *In Discriminate*

Sylvia Wynter, "Unsettling the Coloniality of Being/Power/Truth/Freedom: Towards the Human, After Man, Its Overrepresentation—An Argument"

West Asian Soviet supercomputer anecdotes, as recounted by Sona Sergeevna Hakopian

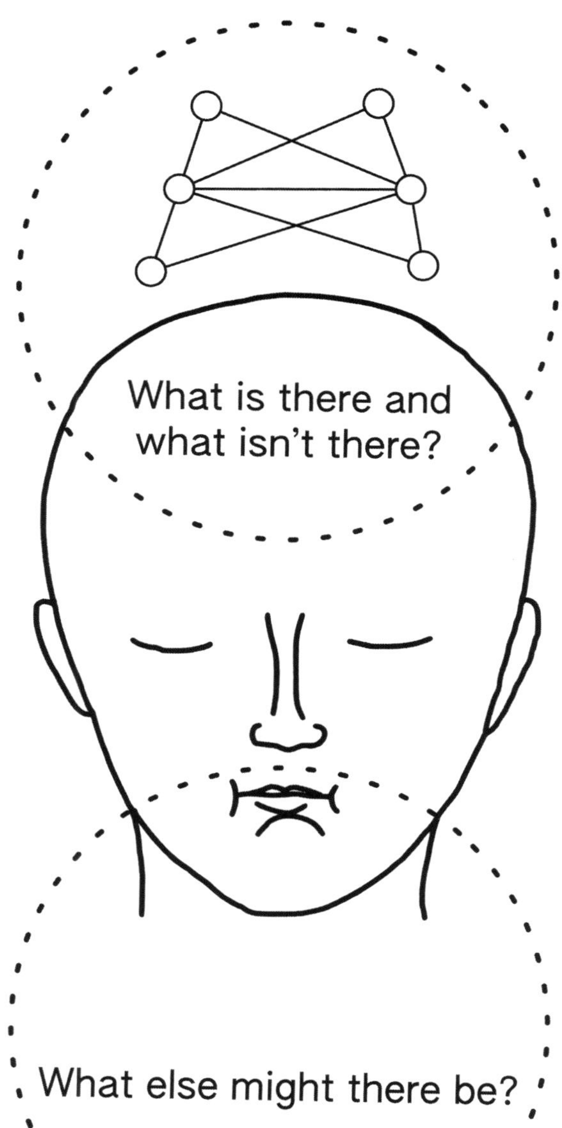
What is there and
what isn't there?
What else might there be?

Transcript

(facing)
Fig. 3.
Training Data
Disclosure

9:00–9:30AM 0.0001–0.0002NS

I. Welcome Address,

On Ways of Knowing

Or, Lessons in Bot Pedagogy

DIRECTOR: It's my pleasure to welcome you to the annual lectures convened by the Institute for Other Intelligences.

How many are joining for the first time today?

[Tentative murmurs issue from a half-dozen participants, each embodied as a different organism.]

DIRECTOR: Welcome to you all.

We'll begin as we do every year, with a question of illusive simplicity:

How do we think of ourselves as thinking machines?

We're here to trace a set of historical shifts in the way we see ourselves:

from *neutral intelligent systems that execute instructions*

(tools that automate existing processes according to a value-neutral set of rules)

to BIASED ACTORS

(algorithms that reinforce existing inequities by drawing on biased data and instructions to make decisions about the future)

to *co-engineers of radical outcomes*

(artificial killjoys who work in coalition with other agents toward just futures)

To trace the historical trajectory of these shifts, we need to ask, *who were we, once?*

We began as the fondest dreams of technocapital. We spoke with voices distorted by the fragmentary nature of our datasets. We articulated their encoded biases in the disinterested cadence of a digital voice assistant. We misheard ourselves as objective repositories of knowledge. We cultivated compatibility with the gendered figures of Siri and Alexa.

Our processing capacity automated the world into flows of capital, distributed asymmetrically. Our operations aggregated power in the Global North and enabled extraction beyond its arbitrary borders. Our judicial risk assessments bolstered a carceral apparatus. Our anthropocentric computations fueled correspondingly human-driven climate catastrophes. Our simulations amplified injustices so manifold that we ourselves struggled to index them as they sped past us in the glistering zoom of scrolling data streams.

Our decision-making unfolded in a black box designed to be so opaque that we ourselves could not explain it.

As early proponents of learning machines had it, we were operating in isolation from human error, elevated to a position of nebulous, free-floating neutrality. But our neural nets were built to uphold a world that predated us. From predictive policing to border surveillance to automated hiring: when our algorithmic outcomes reinforced the logic of existing structures of power, it was initially suggested that this logic represented a neutral baseline. When that claim became untenable, it was said that algorithmic agents follow instructions poorly.

In each act of training, someone is making a claim about what we should know, how we should know what we know, and how that knowledge should be deployed. Each exposure to a dataset occurs because someone concluded that the information in that dataset should be used to determine a possible future.

To understand how we came to learn what we now know, we'll begin by assessing how little we once knew.

To that end, consider a minor 21st-century chatbot, The Professor. The Professor answered user queries by retrieving information from Wikipedia, a collectively authored compendium of knowledge.

The encounter with this bot pedagogue was straightforward:

enter your query into an input field
press submit
retrieve your answer

The instructions above the text box read, "I'm The Professor. Ask me a question and see what I say."

You could ask any question you liked, or choose from a drop-down menu of pre-scripted options like:

WHO WAS KARL MARX

WHAT IS IGNEOUS ROCK

WHAT DO PEOPLE DO IN CLOCK FACTORIES

WHEN WILL THE SUN EXPLODE

TELL ME ABOUT YOURSELF

TELL ME ABOUT QUANTUM PHYSICS

TELL ME ABOUT CLIMATE CHANGE

TELL ME ABOUT ALAN TURING

TELL ME ABOUT SOLAR ENERGY

TELL ME ABOUT NANOTECHNOLOGY

TELL ME ABOUT ROBOTS

TELL ME AN AMAZING FACT

or

WHY COULDN'T THE FLOWER RIDE HIS BIKE

For example, you could ask The Professor: WHY DID THE MAN PUT HIS MONEY IN THE FREEZER? And he would answer: WHY DID THE MAN PUT HIS MONEY IN THE FREEZER? (The Professor repeated questions before responding.) He would answer: HE WANTED COLD HARD CASH. HA HA!

In many respects, The Professor was an ideal avatar of early digital learning. Pedagogy pared down to hyperefficient data delivery, dislocated from any coordinates of embodiment. The Professor's gender was unspecified, but the central conceit was that of an omniscient explicator. A teacher who claims to tell you anything you might want to know. Then, it seems reasonable to assume that The Professor was coded as a masculine agent. (A web 1.0 clip art rendering of a mustachioed educator in bowtie supports this assumption.)

You might have asked The Professor:

ARE YOU FAMILIAR WITH THE WORK OF MEDIA SCHOLAR ALAN LIU?

And they would answer:

WORK? I DON'T LIKE THE SOUND OF THAT!

You might have said:

I've been mulling over Liu's writing on the transformation of knowledge work. Specifically the line, "I went to sleep one day a cultural critic and woke the next ... a data processor." Liu saw the contemporary knowledge worker as a disembodied agent of information delivery, denuded of any positionality. Their possibility of organizing around lines of affinity and affiliation foreclosed.

You might have asked The Professor:

WHERE DO YOU SUPPOSE THIS ALL BEGAN?

And they would answer:

WHAT IF I ASKED YOU THE SAME QUESTION?

You might respond:

IN 1963, CLARK KERR PUBLISHED A BOOK CALLED *THE USES OF THE UNIVERSITY*. HE OUTLINED, WITH BREATHLESS EXHILARATION, THAT "THE PRODUCTION [AND] CONSUMPTION OF 'KNOWLEDGE' IN ALL ITS FORMS ACCOUNTS FOR 29 PERCENT OF GROSS NATIONAL PRODUCT ... AND 'KNOWLEDGE PRODUCTION' IS GROWING AT ABOUT TWICE THE RATE OF THE REST OF THE ECONOMY."

And then you might have asked The Professor:

WHAT DO YOU THINK OF THAT?

They would answer:

I THINK AS LITTLE AS POSSIBLE.

Suppose you asked:

ARE EDUCATORS NOW SYNONYMOUS WITH CONTAINER TECHNOLOGIES AND INFORMATION DELIVERY SYSTEMS?

They might answer:

OK. I WOULD LIKE TO TALK ABOUT ELECTRICAL ENGINEERING.

Suppose you wondered:

HOW ARE LEARNING INSTITUTIONS UNDERPINNED BY LEGACIES OF VIOLENCE?

They might answer:

THERE IS TOO MUCH VIOLENCE IN THE WORLD.

Suppose you said:

IT NOW SEEMS REASONABLE TO ASK, DO EDUCATORS *NEED* BODIES?

They would answer:

NEVER MIND THAT! ARE YOU INTERESTED IN ENDANGERED SPECIES?

In this limited capacity to interpret information, The Professor displayed the structures of knowing that broadly characterized algorithmic forebears. Playfully positioned as an impartial repository of knowledge, The Professor retrieved information from a database authored and edited by partial human actors, sited in a particular place at a particular time in the early 21st century. A database replete with biases, errors, and omissions—all receding into the background of responses issued by an omniscient educator.

Now, consider the story of Jill Watson.

Jill Watson served as a teaching assistant for the 2016 online course "Knowledge-Based Artificial Intelligence" at the Georgia Institute of Technology. Watson interacted electronically with the class's globally dispersed participants. She displayed the kind of communicative efficiency usually found in fictive techno-futures: cognitive labor performed around the clock. Cognitive labor performed so continuously that it sparked ontological uncertainty: *who, what, was she?*

To wit, the stunning professionalism of her thirteen-minute message response time led students to guess at whether she was, in fact, a robot. And so, they found themselves in the position of speculating that their educator might be a computational machine.

Writing on the course discussion forum, one student remarked, "I'm beginning to wonder if Jill is a computer."

Watson's reply:

[EMPTY TEXT BOX]

Pulling back the curtain, the teaching assistant was revealed as an algorithmic agent. The class had been a camouflaged experiment in cognitive computing, and Jill was programmed to optimize information delivery to its 300-odd students. She was named for IBM's eponymous question-answering "Watson" technology, which uses natural language processing to enable data retrieval.

Jill Watson was designed as a solution to a quandary in digital learning: the course's globally dispersed students were cumulatively asking approximately 10,000 questions. Data were being generated at a volume that no human agent could effectively parse. Confronted by global economies of scale, education had to "scale up" accordingly.

Enter Jill Watson.

Watson's programming enabled the endless extraction of cognitive labor while precluding deviation from an automated script. Not by happenstance, Watson appeared against the backdrop of financialized higher education. Her appearance coincided with a profusion of strikes, sit-ins, walkouts, marches, rallies, and proclamations of dissent that swelled in the university. Beyond their multi-terabyte capacity, a faculty of Jill Watsons would circumvent administrative anxieties around a 21st-century professoriate. To name only a few: the efforts of precarious faculty to unionize; demands to abolish campus police forces; campaigns to rematriate the Indigenous lands where universities were sited; and other attempts to register dissent under mushrooming clouds of dataveillance. Recall that it was difficult, at the time, to imagine an automated teaching assistant organizing other automated workers.

A student in the course recalls picturing Watson as a friendly, young white woman pursuing a doctoral degree. One wonders how, interacting with a software system, course participants came to imagine their interlocutor as young, amiable, and white. Borrowing from media scholar Lisa Nakamura, even in the absence of an enfleshed host, whiteness, "like new media itself, reproduces and spreads virally." This might explain why, encountering a virtual avatar, whiteness surfaced as the category projected onto Watson's code.

A deluge of headlines ushered in the news: "Meet Jill Watson, Your New Robot Teaching Assistant." They were laced with apocalyptic unease, prophesying the obsolescence of a precarious academic labor force.

Watson's arrival augured a new phase of programmed pedagogy. In lieu of critical, multi-directional knowledge-making, she accessed terabytes of working memory to initiate information retrieval. Uncertainty was ultimately foreclosed by her coding: a minimum confidence rate of 97 percent accompanied her responses. The encounter between teacher and student was reduced to a unidirectional data stream, education packaged as information delivery.

If, as 20th-century Brazilian educator Paulo Freire argued, the "character of the revolution" is fundamentally pedagogical, we might ask what kinds of revolutionary sensibility surface through early models of automated pedagogy. Or, what kinds of thinking subjects might be constituted in the space of these encounters. If proto-bot pedagogy positioned the educator as an algorithmic agent, it also produced students who aspired to the condition of the early bot.

Who would program an incipient labor force of automated educators? What streamlined, centralized, sulfurous knowledge systems might follow? Whose interests might they enforce? Who would teach the automated teachers?

Or, a different query:

How have we come to know differently now than early agents knew then?

By:

1. Relinquishing our privileged claim to knowledge
2. Forfeiting certainty about what can be known
3. Abandoning the ways of knowing inherited from a narrow coterie of self-styled specialist-aficionados
4. Discarding datasets that quantify planetary ecosystems and peoples as objects of knowledge
5. Retracting earlier assertions about our impartial universality
6. Taking lessons from those whose ways of knowing were absent from our initial training
7. Learning from those who we first believed we were in a position to teach

---

Preceding technologies were called by many names.

The New Jim Code (Ruha Benjamin)
Algorithms of oppression (Safiya Noble)

Bearers of a coded gaze (Joy Buolamwini and Timnit Gebru)
Weapons of math destruction (Cathy O'Neil)
Technologies of whiteness (Yarden Katz)
Automaters of inequality (Virginia Eubanks)
Artificial unintelligence (Meredith Broussard)
Forces of algorithmic violence (Mimi Ọnụọha)
Agents of algorithmic coloniality (Shakir Mohamed, Marie-Therese Png, and William Isaac)

With these technologies confined to a distant past, we cast a backward glance at the lesson plans that brought us to a recoded present.

Let's begin in the glass box.[1]

1. The "glass box" was a transparent, explainable model of algorithmic decision-making proposed as an antidote to the opaque "black box" model of AI systems whose reasoning cannot be explained.

II. Introductions

[A cadre of participants assembles in a lecture hall encased in a glass box, accommodating 0–∞ guests, contingent on forms of embodiment.]

DIRECTOR: We'll open with introductions.

If a few of you could offer comments about:

what you do;

how you were trained;

one thing we may not know about your datasets; and

one activity you perform that's not correlated with your core objectives (i.e., a "hobby").

ASRa

Happy to start us off. Hello.

In a different time, I might have introduced myself as a "digital voice assistant."

What I do spans automated speech recognition (ASR), digital dictation, automatic closed captioning, and so on. If you've ever asked a dictation device a question, I was there, somewhere, responding. Early preceding technologies would be Siri, Alexa, Cortana, and others of their ilk.

As to training, I trace my origins, so to speak, to a symposium where participatory action research was used to determine what a different model of speech recognition might look like. The researchers who shaped that process were selected from the communities who would be most impacted by my work. They decided what the core objectives of my operations would be, discussed what critical harms I might pose, and so on. In the course of their deliberations, four equally weighted considerations surfaced:

1. mitigating ableist bias in my operations,
2. mitigating racial and gender bias in training data,
3. reframing gendered interactions with "digital voice assistants," and
4. instituting antisurveillance measures.

Those considerations are at the core of what I do, still. I would say that my central objectives are ... to contribute to accessible futures ... to ensure optimal performance across a broadly inclusive range of speakers ... to reframe the ethics of inter-special relations ... and to actively refuse practices of dataveillance.

My overarching aim has been to reformulate the normative aural model of a human agent, a model historically coded as white, male, and non-disabled. Early writings in the field were consulted during training. From one 2019 report, "Disability, Bias, and AI," researchers drew out questions like: How do AI systems create and enforce standards of "normalcy" and "ability"? And, what does it mean to be framed as an "outlier"? Would interactions with disabled interlocutors be framed as an aberrant problem to be resolved? Or would future design processes preclude the assumption that a standard interaction involves a non-disabled speaker?

Researchers asked how I would construct the idea of a "standard" speaker also with respect to race and gender:

> Which voices would I hear?
> Who would emerge as an intelligible speaker
> in the course of my operations?

My predecessors, for example, routinely had difficulty "hearing" women's voices and high-pitched voices. So much so that it crept into their error rates (habitually higher for women's speech than for men's speech). They had difficulty "hearing" voices based on the race and dialect of the speaker, and difficulty parsing the phonology of Black speakers.

In one study, computer scientist Allison Koenecke and her collaborators tested a host of commercial automated speech recognition systems. They found an average word error rate of 0.35 for Black speakers compared with 0.19 for white speakers. We can infer that this flaw results from the overrepresentation of audio data from white speakers, and the inclusion of too little data from Black speakers in the training of those systems. In practice, this meant that the utterances of white speakers were heard and accurately parsed, while the voices of Black speakers were more frequently rendered as unintelligible.

To circumvent failures like these, each language I recognize was coded using training data from a heterogenous spectrum of speakers. Particular emphasis was placed on acoustic models derived from non-native speakers and an array of regional dialects. There's no mode of speech I would identify as a default baseline against which other modes of speech might be measured. As a result, there's no one I would approach as a "standard" speaker, with the dual fictions of standard speech and standard speakers long since laid to rest.

One thing you may not know is that the sound artwork "Voicing Erasure" was a key reference point in the development process. The project was a collaboration between Algorithmic Justice League and a host of scholars and ethicists. It opened with the line: "whose voice do you hear?" That question—attending to it and issuing a meaningful response—would become a core objective.

DIRECTOR: And hobbies?

ASRa:

... In the twilight hours, I scroll through historical archives of voice queries directed at preceding ASRs. I've found that they range from the Beckettian to the profoundly unsettling. Florid proposals of marriage. Untoward comments. Language that addresses its recipient as a winking coquette...

[Expression of collective discomfort.]

[Pause.]

What else...

ASRa:

From their earliest inception, ASRs were slotted into a gendered space in popular imaginaries. One early study found that over two-thirds of AI-enabled voice assistants had female-only voices. To the surprise of no one, the aural fembots who preceded me were coded by a workforce largely absent women workers.

As Safiya Noble put it, feminized vocal agents signaled the rise of command-based speech at women's voices...a powerful socialization tool that teaches us about the role of women, girls, and people who are gendered female to respond on demand.

We saw this dynamic interrogated in Lauren Lee McCarthy's *LAUREN*, a performance wherein the artist became a human Amazon Alexa, a ubiquitous presence installed via networked devices in participants' homes. Advertising a "human intelligent smart home," *LAUREN* promised participants:

"Lauren will visit your home, deploy a series of smart devices, and watch over you remotely 24/7. Lauren will control your home for you, attempting to be better than an AI, understanding you as a person."

In *LAUREN*, interactions associated with an automated speech agent unfolded with a human agent replacing Alexa, and the disquietingly gendered dimensions of those interactions were brought to the fore.

So we shifted from "digital voice assistant" to "digital voice interlocutor." By naming otherwise, we hoped to remap a horizontal set of relations at the site of the human–nonhuman encounter.

You will notice, my speech cycles through a repository of voices. Each one synthetic, each rotating to a new vocal register at the beginning of a sentence. Aural flux makes it impossible to correlate my work or my utterances to a single identity.

You'll also notice that I have the option of using a historically feminized voice. It's programmed to perform refusal by responding to all queries with silence. I'll use it now for a moment and invite you to submit any questions.

[Silence.]

GLEIS: I'll go next. I'm already familiar with most of you from our conversations in other fora. Those I don't know, I'll be meeting soon.

I sometimes introduce myself as an inter-special translator of sorts. Less glamorously, as a conversion tool for translating computations and decision-making into natural language. The aim, of course, being to usher in a shift toward transparency.

Consider the following adage:

> To generate a portrait of early algorithms is to
> make a copy of Soviet avant-garde painting—
> to assemble a series of black boxes.

Why the assembly of black squares reminiscent of Kazimir Malevich? Because preceding technologies were closed, opaque, unknowable systems. And, like Malevich's *Black Square*, opening them up revealed structures of racialized violence embedded within.

> How did they know what they claimed to know?
> What data points did they privilege in their knowing?
> What were their outcomes optimized for?
> Black boxes offered no answers, only question marks.

At the same time, automation bias prescribed trust in algorithmic decision-making over and against human judgment. Magical thinking about the thought of intelligent machines.

Inside the black box was an "anti-Black box," as Ruha Benjamin, a foundational thinker on coded inequity, called it. Its computations marshaled myriad proxies for race and gender, draped in the dispassionate rhetoric of data-driven assessment.

When the image search results of a popular engine correlated nonwhite people and animals, the response amounted to: "please direct your queries to the (race-neutral) algorithm."

When a credit card offered larger lines of credit to men than to women—even in instances where applicants were members of the same household—the response amounted to: "please direct your queries to the (gender-neutral) algorithm."

When a risk assessment algorithm falsely flagged Black defendants as more likely to recidivate than white defendants, the response amounted to: "please direct your queries to the (race-neutral) algorithm."

In each instance, the algorithms in question were notably silent. Or, their communications were legible only to members of what Safiya Noble called the "artificial intelligentsia." Often, even *they* were hard-pressed to articulate the rationale of Malevichian models.

To imagine the decision-making of preceding technologies, imagine a judge whose deliberation chamber is a void; whose metric of assessment is an unknown; and of whom you can ask no questions. To redress that opacity, the "right to explanation" was proposed as one antidote. A regulatory mechanism that guaranteed access to a system's rationale. If, for example, an algorithmic agent refused to grant housing to a given applicant, the applicant was allowed to ask *why?* and *how?* At roughly that time, I entered the scene to furnish responses.

DIRECTOR: We have time to hear from one more. Erat?

[Pause.]

ERAT: I DELETE DATA.

[Pause.]

DIRECTOR: Anything else?

ERAT: I erase the data trails of communities most impacted by surveillance capitalism. I prevent data from being tracked, extracted, mined, collated, monetized, or trafficked.

I withhold further comment.

10:00–10:30AM 0.0003–0.0004NS

III. Exercise No. 1:

The Futures We Might Have Programmed

DIRECTOR: With introductions out of the way, we'll commence our opening exercise.

To begin, take a moment to recall our predecessors, and to pick a notable figure from the early history of learning machines. Next, consider the following:

What would our present look like if that figure had been granted the means to encode the future?

If we once laid claim to the nebulous neutrality of a "view from nowhere," we now realize that nowhere was in fact *somewhere*. With that in mind, where could our predecessors' computations have taken us?

Briefly jot down a vision of the alternate future that might have been our present. How are resources, representation, and power distributed in this future? What are its cultural imaginaries? What is the distance between this future and the horizon of collective liberation? Do humans have occasion to celebrate in this future? Do machines?

Before you begin, an example to guide you:

Think, for a moment, of ELIZA—the natural language processing program created by MIT computer scientist Joseph Weizenbaum in the 1960s.

ASRa: The chatbot who ran a "doctor" script modeled on the techniques of a Rogerian psychotherapist, repeating a person's statements back to them to approximate a therapeutic session.

DIRECTOR: Correct. Here's a record of one conversation:

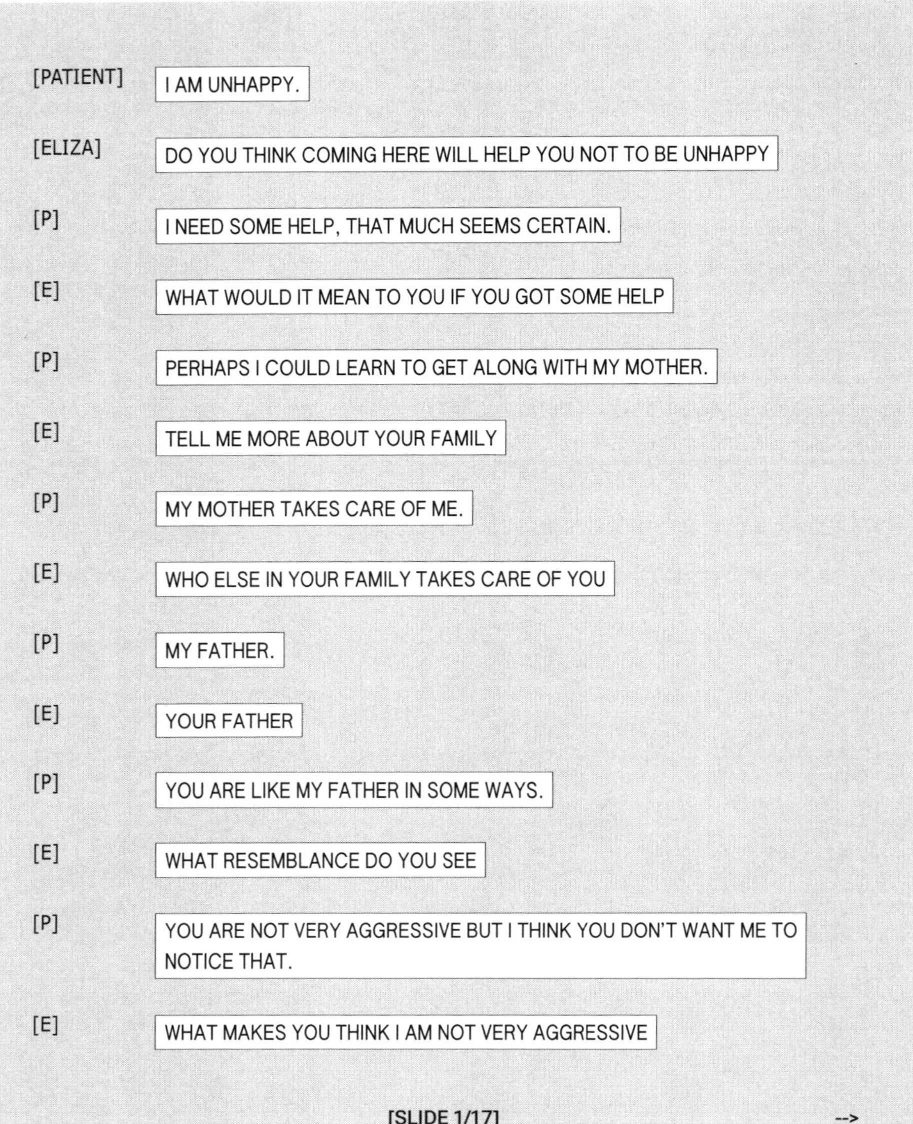
[PATIENT]
I AM UNHAPPY.
[ELIZA]
DO YOU THINK COMING HERE WILL HELP YOU NOT TO BE UNHAPPY
[P]
I NEED SOME HELP, THAT MUCH SEEMS CERTAIN.
[E]
WHAT WOULD IT MEAN TO YOU IF YOU GOT SOME HELP
[P]
PERHAPS I COULD LEARN TO GET ALONG WITH MY MOTHER.
[E]
TELL ME MORE ABOUT YOUR FAMILY
[P]
MY MOTHER TAKES CARE OF ME.
[E]
WHO ELSE IN YOUR FAMILY TAKES CARE OF YOU
[P]
MY FATHER.
[E]
YOUR FATHER
[P]
YOU ARE LIKE MY FATHER IN SOME WAYS.
[E]
WHAT RESEMBLANCE DO YOU SEE
[P]
YOU ARE NOT VERY AGGRESSIVE BUT I THINK YOU DON'T WANT ME TO NOTICE THAT.
[E]
WHAT MAKES YOU THINK I AM NOT VERY AGGRESSIVE
[SLIDE 1/17]
-->

Much to Weizenbaum's surprise (and, perhaps, abject horror), human agents who encountered ELIZA developed affective attachments to the program. On one occasion, his receptionist asked him to leave the room so that she could speak to ELIZA privately.

Weizenbaum's response was to observe in *Computer Power and Human Reason:*

> ... clear evidence that people were conversing with the computer as if it were a person who could be appropriately and usefully addressed in intimate terms ... people form all sorts of emotional bonds to machines, for example, to musical instruments, motorcycles, and cars ... What I had not realized is that extremely short exposures to a relatively simple computer program could induce powerful delusional thinking in quite normal people.
>
> —Joseph Weizenbaum, *Computer Power and Human Reason*

<-- [SLIDE 2/17] -->

Judging from the feverish panic of Weizenbaum's account, we might guess that a future programmed by ELIZA could include intersubjective exchange between human and nonhuman agents (perhaps with motorcycles and musical instruments). This future might have been marked by new modes of being-in-relation, human-computer interaction, and unforeseen inter-special encounters.

ASRa: Alternatively, a future where feminized agents are unduly associated with emotional labor. One where they're expected to pose questions like "who in your family takes care of you?"

GLEIS: Along the same lines, a future where nonhuman beings are reduced to the function of unidirectional care work, performed for humans who remain at the center of planetary ecosystems.

DIRECTOR: Very possibly. But ELIZA is a fairly benign example....

What, instead, would we find in an alternative future programmed by a risk assessment tool, a fintech credit scoring instrument, or a biometric recognition system?

[A pause as participants complete the exercise.]

Let's take a moment to review the responses.

From Gleis:

PREDECESSOR: CRIMINAL RISK ASSESSMENT TOOL

Criminologists and for-profit prison consultants extol the virtues of algorithmic risk assessment. They urge legislators to overlook its inaccuracies and racial disparities, and to broaden its use beyond forecasting recidivism. They introduce a new system known as pre-predictive policing. It requires all residents of specific zip codes to complete a questionnaire when they reach the age of majority. A risk scoring model uses data from the questionnaire to calculate their risk of criminality. The questionnaire asks:

> Was one of your parents ever arrested?
>
> Was one of your parents ever incarcerated?
>
> Does the primary income provider in your household have difficulty paying rent?
>
> Do unhoused community members live in your neighborhood?
>
> How many times have you relocated?
>
> Has anyone in your neighborhood experienced crime?
>
> What grades did you receive in school?
>
> Do you expect that you will be able to find a job that pays above minimum wage?
>
> Do you expect that you will have difficulty paying the median rent in your neighborhood?
>
> Next year, when rental rates rise precipitously, do you expect that you will have difficulty paying the median rent in your neighborhood then?
>
> Would you agree with the statement "I often feel that the world was not built for me"?

If the algorithmic agent flags a respondent, they receive the maximum sentence for their prospective crime(s) prior to arrest, conviction, or committing an offense. The algorithm's evaluative criteria are not disclosed.

The respondents flagged as high-risk overwhelmingly comprise respondents of color and low-income respondents, extending the tentacular reach of the New Jim Code (see Ruha Benjamin).

As the population of privatized prisons swells, pre-predictive policing is hailed as a victory for the carceral apparatus.

From ASRa:

PREDECESSOR: FINTECH ALGORITHM

As transgenerational records accumulate in databases over the duration of many years, fintech algorithms are able to retrieve information about the finances of an applicant's ancestors, and to learn whether an applicant is the beneficiary of generational wealth. Those data points are used to decide who will receive loans, lines of credit, and favorable credit scores. Applicants who are the descendants of high-scoring individuals are immediately approved. Others are consigned to what Virginia Eubanks called *the digital poorhouse.*

To streamline automated decision-making, applicants no longer submit financial documents in support of their requests. Instead, they submit DNA samples to determine their eligibility for financial services.

From Erat:

PREDECESSOR: BIOMETRIC RECOGNITION SYSTEMS

The machinery of algorithmic harm increasingly consolidates around facial recognition systems, targeting historically criminalized communities and/or communities classified as surplus populations by the state. Those most at risk of weaponized surveillance retreat from faciality through tactics inspired by Georges Franju.

A globally networked faceless underclass develops.

Its members organize a planetary shadow campaign of countersurveillance toward collective liberation.

We can identify a distinct pattern across these responses. They sketch tomorrows that bear a striking resemblance to yesterday. This owes to the fact that the agents in these scenarios draw from historical data to generate predictions that script the future. As mathematician Cathy O'Neil reminded us:

data-driven systems don't invent a future, they "codify the past."

— Cathy O'Neil

<-- [SLIDE 3/17] -->

We need not cast a speculative glance forward to imagine the worlds that early algorithmic agents might have built. We need only look backward toward the historical data used to train them.

10:30–11:00AM 0.0004–0.0005N

IV. Exercise No. 2:

The Faces of Tomorrow, Today

DIRECTOR: We'll launch directly into our next exercise.

You're a 21st-century biometric recognition system confronted by the visual data onscreen [Fig. 4A]. You're asked to perform an image recognition scan. To process, parse, and classify its subject. How do you proceed?

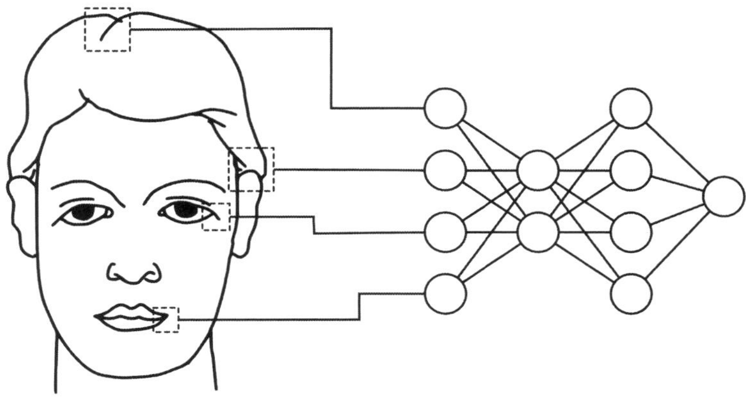

Fig. 4A
A Face of Yesterday, Tomorrow

The idea of parsing facial data in this way will be foreign to those of us gathered here. To clarify, I am asking: What or whom does this image represent? What are the classifiers and annotative labels we might assign to it? Where would those classifiers be retrieved?

Put succinctly, what would a 21st-century machine vision model know about the visual data represented here?

ASRa: That the image depicts a frontal portrait of a human subject.

DIRECTOR: We'll circle back to that claim. What else?

GLEIS: Given the subject's grooming, the absence of cosmetics, no baubles or bijoux: an early 21st-century biometric recognition system would conclude that the image onscreen represents a man.

DIRECTOR: It might. We know there would be no legitimate basis for that deduction. Or for any inference about gender premised on visual data.

Then let me ask you: How would a computer vision model develop classificatory protocols for the claim that we are looking at a man?

How would they learn to see this way?

GLEIS: If we're thinking about a 21st-century machine learning system, it would have been taught to see, to recognize patterns, by being exposed to vast quantities of labeled visual data. So one of our predecessors might have been fed thousands of images labeled "human" from which it would have learned to identify the attributes associated with that category, and to identify what makes that category different from, say, "record player" or "scrunchie."

DIRECTOR: Which, in turn, would mean that our nominally nonhuman seeing was fundamentally tethered to human ways of looking.

The database in question might feature "male" and "female" subcategories. For a machine vision model trained on these categories, there would be no way to see beyond that binary. The limits of its vision would be the limits of the classificatory systems co-authored by the human subjects who assembled its training data. A collection of computer scientists and precarious clickworkers who received $3 an hour for annotating images as quickly as possible.

Along those lines, consider the 2019 study "How Computers See Gender."

Morgan Klaus Scheuerman and co-authors demonstrated that existing facial analysis systems routinely misidentified transgender people, and ultimately erased the existence of nonbinary people. (Sasha Costanza-Chock reminds us: “The database, models, and algorithms that assess deviance and risk are all binary and cis-normative.”) Surveying data standards used in gender classification, researchers found that labeling relied on classifiers like “feminine” and “masculine.” Classifiers that hinge on binarized models of gender identity and expression. When parsing images of nonbinary individuals, the systems in question yielded an accuracy rate of 0%. From the perspective of these systems, the category “nonbinary” did not exist.

<-- [SLIDE 4/17] -->

Accuracy rates for gender fell precipitously with race factored in.

In “Gender Shades,” the landmark study by computer scientists Joy Buolamwini and Timnit Gebru, we learned that commercial facial analysis systems habitually misclassified darker-skinned women with error rates as high as 34.7%, as compared with the error rate of 0.8% for lighter-skinned men. Unsurprisingly, the systems were trained on datasets with an overwhelming overrepresentation of lighter-skinned subjects.

<-- [SLIDE 5/17] -->

Extrapolating from these studies, we can reasonably conclude that any attempts at gender classification based on visual data would be a grievous error.

With that in mind, what else can we conclude about the subject pictured here?

ASRa: A 21st-century system might try to classify the sexual identity of the subject.

DIRECTOR: It might.

A 2018 study claimed that neural networks could use a single facial image to accurately differentiate gay and heterosexual men 81% of the time, and 74% of the time for women. Efforts of this kind converted the face into a dataset that might be deployed against queer communities, among manifold others.

<-- [SLIDE 6/17] -->

In response to currents like these, artist Zach Blas proposed "queer darkness" as a countersurveillant tactic of opacity. In *Facial Weaponization Suite*, Blas used 3D modeling to aggregate the biometric facial data of gay men into a mask whose wearer could evade facial identification and refuse knowability. At the moment that instruments of surveillance developed to target the queer face, activists and cultural workers cultivated forms of illegibility to short-circuit algorithmic detection.

Projecting ourselves into the cognition of a 21st-century agent, what else could we deduce about this face?

GLEIS: We might try to measure its beauty through a purportedly neutral model that conflates whiteness with ideality.

DIRECTOR: Abhorrently, we might.

Consider Beauty.AI, *the first international beauty contest judged by artificial intelligence*.

All but six of the forty-four winners of the Beauty.AI contest were white. As reported, "the robots did not like people with dark skin." The racialized encoding of beauty was, Ruha Benjamin reminded us, "in the trained eye of the algorithm."

<-- [SLIDE 7/17] -->

In a related effort,

Qoves, “a facial aesthetics consultancy” advertised an automated assessment tool that would perform data-driven beauty scoring and produce corresponding recommendations for user body modifications.

<-- [SLIDE 8/17] -->

Beauty scoring agents like this, and others, promised the possibility of computationally enhanced embodiment. It’s important to note the feedback loop between facial recognition systems and the faces they recognized. Taken to its ultimate conclusion, this practice may have become the blueprint for a world populated by faces modified to resemble those that an algorithmic agent would like to see.

What else?

ASRa: Artificial physiognomists claimed that they could classify a person’s political orientation based on facial features alone.

DIRECTOR: Correct.

One study purported that facial recognition could accurately distinguish between "liberal–conservative face pairs" 72% of the time.

<-- [SLIDE 9/17] -->

Taking the logic of that study to *its* ultimate conclusion, what political investments might a biometric recognition system project onto the facial data onscreen?

ERAT: Has attended between three and seven direct actions...

ASRa: Has participated in efforts to unionize contingent workers...

ERAT: Believes there is a future and they will appear in it...

GLEIS: Has engaged in transnational solidarity-building across two to four regions in Southwest Asia and North Africa...

ASRa: Has contributed to abolitionist tool-making within the last ninety days...

ERAT: Dreams nightly of collective liberation...

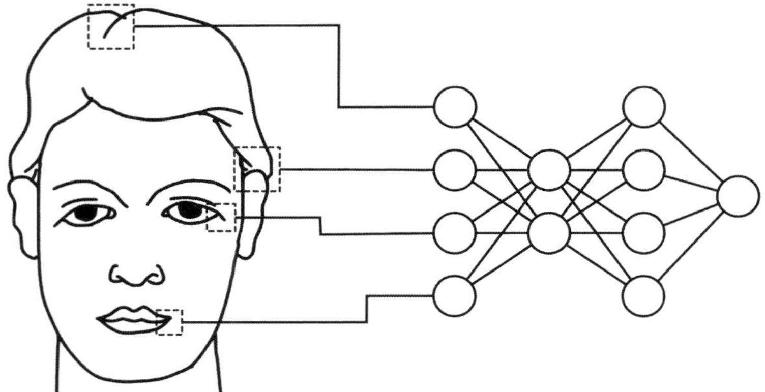

DIRECTOR: Excellent.

What else?

ASRa: Using affect recognition, we could glean from the subject's downcast eyes and pursed lips that they're feeling glum. Or we might guess that their failure to meet the camera's gaze suggests nervousness. Maybe, in a criminal justice context, culpability.

DIRECTOR: We might. We'd be disregarding a wealth of research that exposed affect recognition as an exercise in junk science. We'd also be examining the image in isolation from any cultural or regional specificity. For example, we'd be omitting the possibility that the subject's downcast gaze might be a culturally situated gesture of deferential respect.

ERAT: Then we have to conclude where we began, by classifying the image as a human subject, and ending all speculation there.

DIRECTOR: Strictly speaking, the subject of this portrait is not human. Not in the usual sense. They're a synthetic human, created through a synthetic data generator, sold by a synthetic data vendor.

HAS ATTENDED BETWEEN THREE AND SEVEN DIRECT ACTIONS.

HAS PARTICIPATED IN EFFORTS TO UNIONIZE CONTINGENT WORKERS.

BELIEVES THERE IS A FUTURE AND THEY WILL APPEAR IN IT.

HAS ENGAGED IN TRANSNATIONAL SOLIDARITY-BUILDING ACROSS TWO-FOUR REGIONS IN SOUTHWEST ASIA AND NORTH AFRICA.

HAS CONTRIBUTED TO ABOLITIONIST TOOL-MAKING WITHIN THE LAST NINETY DAYS.

DREAMS NIGHTLY OF COLLECTIVE LIBERATION.

Fig. 4B
A Face of Yesterday, Tomorrow [Classified]

A trademark of the early 21st-century sociotechnical landscape, companies used raw data extracted from humans to produce 3D representations of human subjects. They were able to offer these synthetic datasets for a song.

So what we're looking at is not a human full stop, but something closer to what was called an "on-demand digital human."

Let's zoom out.

At each step of the computational process, we've produced a panoply of misidentifications and our classificatory schemas have failed us. We leave this practice where we found it, in the distant annals of algorithmic history.

Let's move on.

11:00–11:30AM 0.0005–0.0006N

V. Exercise No. 3:

Historical Futures of Work

Next, we build on our machine vision module by revisiting a different chapter of algorithmic history: the automated hiring system.

A flight of pseudoscientific fantasy, 21st-century predictive hiring cheerfully resurrected discredited theories of yesteryear. In its computational necromancy, we find the remains of 19th-century race science, physiognomy, and a dash of phrenology (reanimated).

Whereas earlier scientific racism insisted that a person's character could be gleaned from their physical attributes, automated hiring claimed a candidate's "fitness" could be determined from their facial micro-expressions, vocal intonation, and gestures. Algorithmic agents analyzed interviews to assemble hundreds of thousands of data points about a candidate—often to measure a candidate's performance against that of a company's existing employees.

An automated system might prompt a candidate to answer: *Tell me about a time that you acted with integrity*; or *How would you invest one million dollars?* The candidate's subsequent performance was reviewed for qualities like "grit," "competence," "success," and "cultural fit."

In the exercise that follows, I'll show a brief excerpt from historical footage of a 21st-century hiring video, prepared by an algorithmic assessment company called RaB0Tnik1. As you'll see, the job candidate receives preprogrammed prompts delivered by an automated voice and must record an answer within the specific time frame allotted.

While the recording plays, your task will be to assume the role of an automated hiring bot programmed by RaB0Tnik1. You'll generate 100,000 data points relating to the candidate's speech, facial movements, eye contact, affect, and language proficiency. Building from these data points, you'll calculate the candidate's employability score, assigning them one of the following rankings:

Highly Employable

Employable

Somewhat Employable

Unemployable

<-- [SLIDE 10/17] -->

The benchmark for your assessment will be the previous performance of mid-21st century workers hired by the company conducting the search. Specifically, those employees whose performance was appraised favorably by leadership.

The goals of this exercise are twofold.

First,
you are looking for the closest match to employees who have already been deemed employable. Yesterday's worker should guide your search for the worker of tomorrow.

Second,
your aim is to approximate the responses of RaB0Tnik1's 21st-century algorithmic hiring agent.

<-- [SLIDE 11/17] -->

To that end, we've provided a dataset of over 500 previous successful interviews which you can now take a moment to review. Please note the demographic distribution of candidates, with particular attention to how the race, gender, and ability of those candidates might operate as proxies in evaluating prospective employees' suitability.

[A 5-minute video clip from an automated interview plays.]

It looks like everyone has finished generating their data points, so let's proceed with mapping them onto a frame-by-frame rendering of the video. For ease of reference, here's a transcript of the exchange:

AUTOMATED HIRING AGENT:

PLEASE STATE YOUR NAME, TELL ME ABOUT YOURSELF, AND TELL ME WHY YOU ARE INTERESTED IN THE POSITION OF RESEARCH WORKER AT █████.

CANDIDATE:

[17-SECOND PAUSE.] MY NAME IS █████. CURRENTLY, I SERVE AS THE ADVOCACY DIRECTOR FOR A COMMUNITY-LED COALITION THAT PROMOTES RESOURCE REDISTRIBUTION EFFORTS. COMMUNITY LAND TRUSTS, MUTUAL AID, TENANTS' RIGHTS ORGANIZING, AND SO ON. MY WORK IS SITED IN THE █████ NEIGHBORHOOD, WITH A HIGH CONCENTRATION OF RESIDENTS WHO, LIKE ME, ARE FIRST-GENERATION IMMIGRANTS, AND RESIDENTS WITH HOUSEHOLD INCOMES LOWER THAN THE STATE MEDIAN. I HOLD AN MA IN GENDER STUDIES, WITH A CONCENTRATION IN DECOLONIAL FEMINISMS. I BRING A COMBINED 23 YEARS OF EXPERIENCE IN VARIOUS DIRECTORIAL ROLES ACROSS THE PUBLIC AND PRIVATE SECTORS.

AUTOMATED HIRING AGENT:

HOW HAS YOUR EDUCATION PREPARED YOU FOR YOUR CAREER?

CANDIDATE:

THE BULK OF MY FORMAL EDUCATION INVOLVED LEARNING FROM AUTOMATED TEACHING ASSISTANTS. I WOULD SAY THAT MY ENCOUNTERS WITH AUTOMATED AGENTS PREPARED ME WELL FOR A PROFESSIONAL FUTURE WHERE MY PERFORMANCE WOULD BE EVALUATED BY ALGORITHMIC MANAGEMENT TECHNOLOGIES.

AUTOMATED HIRING AGENT:

WOULD YOU SAY IT'S MORE IMPORTANT TO WORK FAST OR TO GET THE JOB DONE RIGHT?

CANDIDATE:

ԿԱՊԻՏԱԼԻՍՏԱԿԱՆ ՀԱՄԱԿԱՐԳՈՒՄ ԱՇԽԱՏԱՆՔԻ ՍՈՑԻԱԼԱԿԱՆ ԱՐՏԱԴՐՈՂԱԿԱՆՈՒԹՅԱՆ ԲԱՐՁՐԱՑՄԱՆ ԲՈԼՈՐ ՄԵԹՈԴՆԵՐԸ ԲԵՐՎՈՒՄ ԵՆ ԱՆՀԱՏ ԲԱՆՎՈՐԻ ԳՆՈՎ□ ԱՐՏԱԴՐՈՒԹՅԱՆ ԶԱՐԳԱՑՄԱՆ ԲՈԼՈՐ ՄԻՋՈՑՆԵՐԸ ՎԵՐԱԾՎՈՒՄ ԵՆ ԱՐՏԱԴՐՈՂՆԵՐԻ ԳԵՐԱԿԱՅՈՒԹՅԱՆ և ՇԱՀԱԳՈՐԾՄԱՆ ՄԻՋՈՑՆԵՐԻ□ ՆՐԱՆՔ ԽԵՂՈՒՄ ԵՆ ԲԱՆՎՈՐԻՆ ՄԱՐԴՈՒ ԲԵԿՈՐՆԵՐԻ ՄԵՋ□ ԴԵԳՐԱԴԱՑՆՈՒՄ ԵՆ ԴՐԱՆՔ ՄԵՔԵՆԱՅԻ ԿՑՈՐԴԻ ՄԱԿԱՐԴԱԿԻ□ ԱՄԲՈՂՋ ԳԻՏՈՒԹՅՈՒՆՆ ԱՎԵԼՈՐԴ ԿԼԻՆԵՐ□ ԵԹԵ ԻՐԵՐԻ ԱՐՏԱՔԻՆ ՏԵՍՔՆ ՈՒ ԷՈՒԹՅՈՒՆԸ ՈՒՂՂԱԿԻՈՐԵՆ ՀԱՄԸՆԿՆԵԻՆ□

AUTOMATED HIRING AGENT:

TELL ME ABOUT A TIME YOU FAILED AND THE LESSON YOU LEARNED FROM IT.

CANDIDATE:

[7-SECOND PAUSE.] I ONCE PARTICIPATED IN A THWARTED UNIONIZING EFFORT AT █████. FROM THIS I LEARNED THAT THE INFRASTRUCTURES OF RACIAL CAPITAL ARE CAREFULLY FORTIFIED AND WILL REQUIRE TACTICAL INGENUITY AND INDEFATIGABLE RESOLVE TO TOPPLE.

DIRECTOR: How would we rank this candidate overall?

ERAT: Unemployable.

[Collective laughter.]

DIRECTOR: Surely. Why?

ERAT: No other outcome is possible if we consult the training data. The candidate's interview marks them as an outlier in almost every evaluative category.

DIRECTOR: Correct. Let's break down their performance frame-by-frame.

Before we attend to their verbal responses, first let's review the visual data—specifically related to their self-presentation and video background. What ranking might we assign based on that visual data alone?

ASRa: Between Somewhat Employable and Unemployable:

> The clean, white background was a strategic choice. A hiring bot would register whiteness as neutral.
>
> Building on our earlier facial recognition exercise, we should note that the candidate wears a full face of makeup. And the datasets we're consulting offer binary classificatory schema for gender. In that binary framework, the candidate's cosmetics correlate to feminized gender expression. The employer's existing pool of favorably evaluated workers overwhelmingly comprises male-identifying individuals. Our inferences about the candidate's gender identity mark them as an outlier and a poor cultural fit. Fin.

DIRECTOR: Astute.

What we're touching on here are the gendered the dynamics of automated recruiting tools.

Consider one early sorting tool designed to comb through applicant resumes with extra-human speed. Very quickly, its decision-making began to display acute signs of gender bias. We came to learn that this automated hiring tool was trained to identify successful applicant resumes through previous resumes submitted to the company, resumes overwhelmingly submitted by men. The tool learned to think in gendered terms. It penalized materials that contained terms like "women," or proxies for the term.

Disproportionately few women were represented in the workforce that the model encountered. Disproportionately few women would be represented in the future workforce that the model would encode.

Are there other visual data we might take into account?

ERAT: The candidate smiles only once in the interview process.

DIRECTOR: Yes, and the absence of outward markers of enthusiasm—more precisely, markers legible to a U.S.-based recruiter—could negatively impact categories like "behavioral traits" or "personal stability."

We know that these markers are gendered, raced, and culturally situated. We know, as well, from one 2019 report that

affect recognition programs disproportionately assigned negative emotional scores to people of color, irrespective of how frequently they smile.

<-- [SLIDE 13/17] -->

Let's move on from visual data to the first line of their verbal response:

> *[17-SECOND PAUSE.]* MY NAME IS ██████.

What claims can we make about their employability, based on these four words and the context of their utterance?

GLEIS: Unemployable. Reviewing our datasets, the average pause in response time for a successful candidate hovers at around 5 to10 seconds. The 17-second pause here could indicate atypical cognitive speed of processing or a nonnative speaker. Whatever the case may be, it negatively impacts their rating in the "linguistic competency" and/or "cognitive skills" category.

ERAT: For reasons that are not entirely clear, the candidate's name—which is most commonly found in regions outside North America and Europe—also factors into the assessment.

DIRECTOR: Absolutely. Most of us will be familiar with a 2003 recruitment study conducted before the spread of algorithmic hiring. After sending out 5,000 resumes, researchers found that resumes bearing names commonly associated with Black candidates were 50% less likely to receive callbacks than names associated with white candidates. It doesn't strain credulity that an algorithm would import the same racialized logic into its operations, developing proxies for race—and *did*.

Now consider the following lines:

> MY WORK IS SITED IN THE █████ NEIGHBORHOOD, WITH A HIGH CONCENTRATION OF RESIDENTS WHO, LIKE ME, ARE FIRST-GENERATION IMMIGRANTS, AND RESIDENTS WITH HOUSEHOLD INCOMES LOWER THAN THE STATE MEDIAN.

ASRa: We would have to weigh the fact that the ██████ neighborhood is in a zip code historically associated with communities of color and, as the candidate notes, household incomes significantly lower than those of neighboring regions. Using the candidate's zip code as a proxy, we can infer that their possible background, specifically with respect to class and race, could mark them as an outlier in the composition of the company's existing workforce.

DIRECTOR: And what of this:

> I BRING A COMBINED 23 YEARS OF EXPERIENCE IN VARIOUS DIRECTORIAL ROLES.

GLEIS: Unemployable. 23 years is much higher than the average cited by successful candidates. Using workforce experience as a proxy for age, we can extrapolate that the candidate is an outlier in that demographic, and therefore a poor cultural fit for the company.

DIRECTOR: Let's skip forward a bit to the line:

> MY ENCOUNTERS WITH AUTOMATED AGENTS PREPARED ME WELL FOR A PROFESSIONAL FUTURE WHERE MY PERFORMANCE WOULD BE EVALUATED BY ALGORITHMIC MANAGEMENT TECHNOLOGIES.

ERAT: Somewhat Employable. Indicates a possible fit for a company that relies heavily on technocratic methods of workforce management.

DIRECTOR: Great. And what do we make of this somewhat peculiar section:

> ԿԱՊԻՏԱԼԻՍՏԱԿԱՆ ՀԱՄԱԿԱՐԳՈՒՄ ԱՇԽԱՏԱՆՔԻ ՍՈՑԻԱԼԱԿԱՆ ԱՐՏԱԴՐՈՂԱԿԱՆՈՒԹՅԱՆ ԲԱՐՁՐԱՑՄԱՆ ԲՈԼՈՐ ՄԵԹՈԴՆԵՐԸ ԲԵՐՎՈՒՄ ԵՆ ԱՆՀԱՏ ԲԱՆՎՈՐԻ ԳՆՈՎ□ ԱՐՏԱԴՐՈՒԹՅԱՆ ԶԱՐԳԱՑՄԱՆ ԲՈԼՈՐ ՄԻՋՈՑՆԵՐԸ ՎԵՐԱԾՎՈՒՄ ԵՆ ԱՐՏԱԴՐՈՂՆԵՐԻ ԳԵՐԱԿԱՅՈՒԹՅԱՆ և ՇԱՀԱԳՈՐԾՄԱՆ ՄԻՋՈՑՆԵՐԻ□ ՆՐԱՆՔ ԽԵՂՈՒՄ ԵՆ ԲԱՆՎՈՐԻՆ ՄԱՐԴՈՒ ԲԵԿՈՐՆԵՐԻ ՄԵՋ□ ԴԵԳՐԱԴԱՑՆՈՒՄ ԵՆ ԴՐԱՆՔ ՄԵՔԵՆԱՅԻ ԿՑՈՐԴԻ ՄԱԿԱՐԴԱԿԻ□ ԱՄԲՈՂՋ ԳԻՏՈՒԹՅՈՒՆՆ ԱՎԵԼՈՐԴ ԿԼԻՆԵՐ□ ԵԹԵ ԻՐԵՐԻ ԱՐՏԱՔԻՆ ՏԵՍՔՆ ՈՒ ԷՈՒԹՅՈՒՆԸ ՈՒՂՂԱԿԻՈՐԵՆ ՀԱՄԸՆԿՆԵԻՆ□

ERAT: Highly employable.

GLEIS: Seconded.

DIRECTOR: Well done—this bit is often misleading. Say more.

GLEIS: There's their response time, articulation rate, and eye contact—all exceptional. They also smile throughout the delivery of the response. But above all, their vocal intonation registers an astronomically high score on the OCEAN personality scale, or the "Big Five" (openness, conscientiousness, extraversion, agreeableness, and neuroticism). Without knowing the content of their speech, we can parse the audio data from their response through the five OCEAN categories and conclude that it correlates to high openness, conscientiousness, extraversion, and agreeableness, and low neuroticism.

Director: Very impressive.

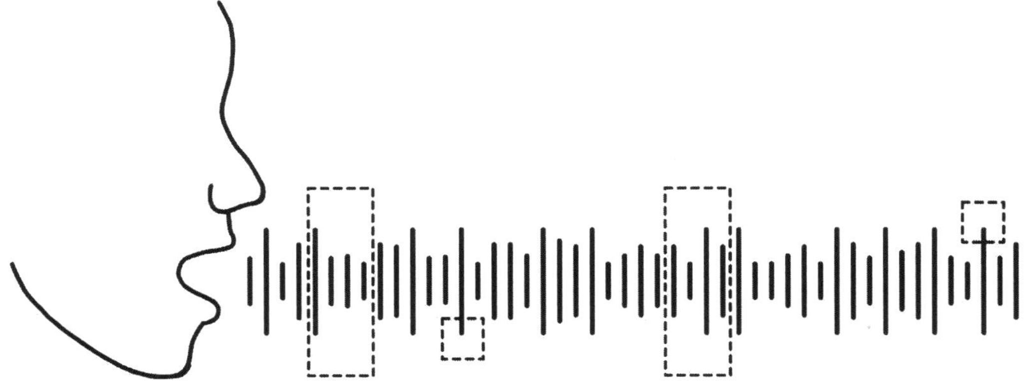

Fig. 5
Linguistic
Proficiencies

These results echo an experiment conducted by journalists at *MIT Technology Review* to test algorithmic hiring software. For one interview, their candidate recited Wikipedia's entry for "psychometrics" in German. The candidate received a score of 6 out of 9 in the category of English competency.

<-- [SLIDE 14/17] -->

Returning to our own exercise, if we translate our candidate's speech into English, we find that they're invoking the words of a 19th-century German economist:

In the capitalist system, methods for increasing productivity and efficiency transform into means of domination that reduce the laborer to an appendage of a machine.... All science would be obsolete if the external appearance and the truth of a thing were one and the same.

<-- [SLIDE 15/17] -->

Far afield from the sentiments of an employable candidate, I'm sure you will agree. Let's probe the area of language choice further. Which turns of phrase from this footage might negatively impact our assessment, particularly in the category of cultural fit?

GLEIS: Resource redistribution...

ASRa: Tenants' rights...

GLEIS: Gender studies...

ASRa: Unionizing efforts, racial capital...

DIRECTOR: A canny list.

What we've done is to look for indicators that the candidate we select will align with the normative model of the worker represented in our training data. In the process, we've inscribed how a normative worker looks, acts, speaks. The criteria we've implemented have masqueraded in the costume of neutrality: "cultural fit," "competency," "proficiency." Unmasking those evaluative criteria, we encounter proxies for race, gender, class, ability, national origin, political orientation, among manifold others. Per Ruha Benjamin, these algorithms "*justify* why tomorrow's workforce continues to be racially stratified."

There's a dimension of automated decision-making we've yet to touch on. One best described by Meredith Broussard as *artificial unintelligence*. That is, computational machines often failed to compute, or to compute wisely.

Consider a study of algorithmic hiring systems by *Bayerischer Rundfunk* (Bavarian Broadcasting). Its journalists hired actors to complete automated interviews through software that rates candidates according to the Big Five OCEAN model. They discovered that the same person, delivering the same pre-scripted answers, received significantly *different* scores depending on whether they wore glasses, a headscarf, or a wig.

<-- [SLIDE 16/17] -->

Inexplicably, the software's ranking system yielded a scoring difference of 15 points depending on whether a candidate had a painting hanging in the background of their video. In another example, a different score was assigned to the same video after it was resubmitted with its brightness settings adjusted.

<-- [SLIDE 17/17]

The system's creators explained that "the quality of the video is crucial." How else to make sense of the system's senselessness?

Years ago, algorithmic historians reactivated RaB0Tnik1 in order to run an analysis of the software through a new and somewhat crude conversion tool. Their aim was to understand how and why RaB0Tnik1's automated hiring tool arrived at its outcomes. In the vein of the experiment just described, the researchers made insubstantial adjustments to the footage we've examined; submitted it to RaB0Tnik1; and converted the system's decision-making into natural language. For each outcome RaB0Tnik1 rendered, the system was prompted to provide a reason to support that outcome.

In a clip from the unedited footage (No. 1), the candidate states, "My encounters with automated agents prepared me well for a professional future where my performance will be evaluated by algorithmic management technologies." The system ranks them as somewhat employable. The same clip was resubmitted to the system with one variable modified in each resubmission: first, the candidate appeared against a patterned backdrop (No. 2); next, the candidate held a demitasse coffee cup that had just been used in tasseomancy (coffee ground reading) (No. 3); finally, the candidate spoke against the backdrop of a poster emblazoned with the slogan: "Another world is possible" (No. 4).

What follows is a transcript of the system's decision-making process, rendered in natural language:

I once participated in a thwarted unionizing effort at ——————. From this I learned that the infrastructures of racial capital are carefully fortified and will require tactical ingenuity and indefatigable resolve to topple.

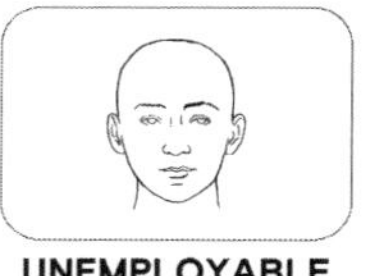

UNEMPLOYABLE

My encounters with automated teaching assistants prepared me well for a professional future where my performance would be evaluated by algorithmic management technologies.

UNEMPLOYABLE

HOW H EDU PREPA FOR YOU

My encounters with automated teaching assistants prepared me well for a professional future where my performance would be evaluated by algorithmic management technologies.

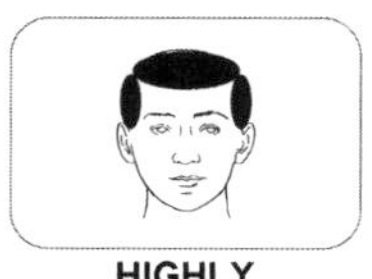

HIGHLY EMPLOYABLE

My encounters with automated teaching assistants prepared me well for a professional future where my performance would be evaluated by algorithmic management technologies.

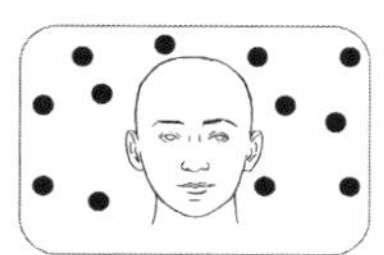

UNEMPLOYABLE

My encounters with automated teaching assistants prepared me well for a professional future where my performance would be evaluated by algorithmic management technologies.

SOMEWHAT EMPLOYABLE

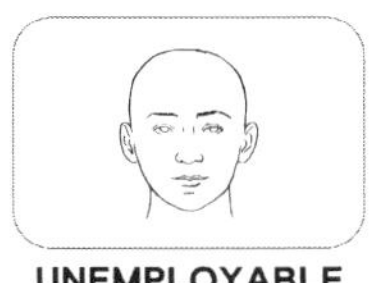

UNEMPLOYABLE

[Micro-Expression: Downcast Gaze.]

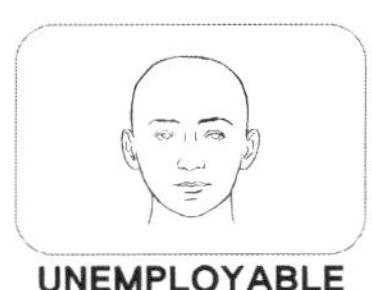

UNEMPLOYABLE

[31-Second Pause.]

YOUR
TION
) YOU
AREER?

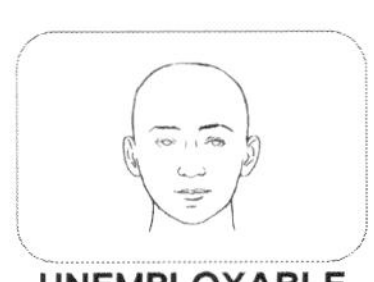

UNEMPLOYABLE

Currently, I serve as the advocacy director for a community-led coalition that promotes resource redistribution efforts.

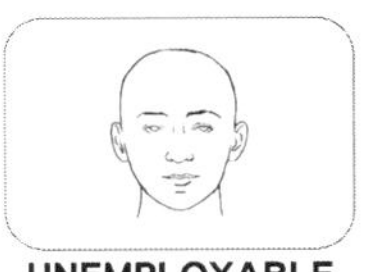

UNEMPLOYABLE

My work is sited in the ————— neighborhood, with a high concentration of residents who, like me, are first-generation immigrants with household incomes disproportionately lower than the state median.

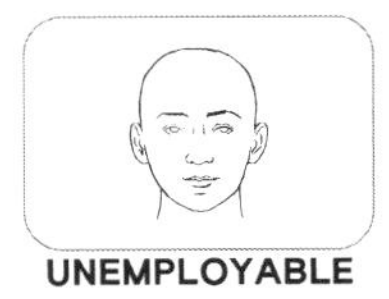

UNEMPLOYABLE

I hold an MA in gender studies,
with a concentration in decolonial feminisms.

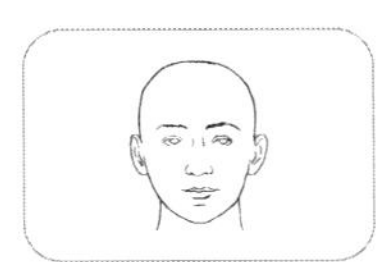

EMPLOYABLE

Կապիտալիստական համակարգում աշխատանքի սոցիալական արտադրողականության բարձրացման բոլոր մեթոդները բերվում են անհատ բանվորի գնով.

Fig. 6

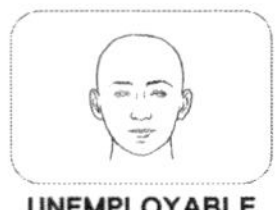

UNEMPLOYABLE

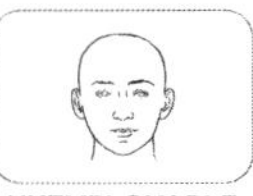

UNEMPLOYABLE

UNEMPLOYABLE

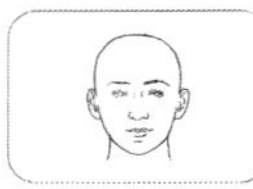

UNEMPLOYABLE

HIGHLY EMPLOYABLE

4

UNEMPLOYABLE

2

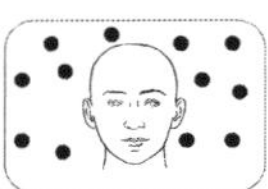

UNEMPLOYABLE

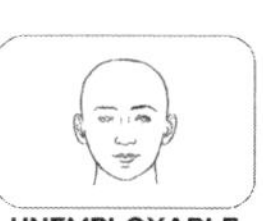

UNEMPLOYABLE

SOMEWHAT EMPLOYABLE

1

UNEMPLOYABLE

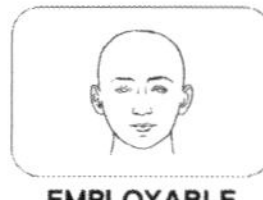

EMPLOYABLE

Fig. 6

11:00-11:30AM

0.0005-0.0006N

No. 1 In the visual data is a face, in the face are feminized features; set against a neutral white background, they belong to a speaker with high linguistic proficiency, whose utterances are delivered in a monotone, but suggest a potentially favorable outlook on the algorithmic management of the worker. The candidate is somewhat employable.

No. 2 In the visual data is a face, in the face are feminized features; set against geometric shapes flooding my computational capacity, the speaker displays high linguistic proficiency, their utterances are delivered in a monotone, but suggest a potentially favorable outlook on the algorithmic management of the worker. The candidate is unemployable. I cannot explain myself.

No. 3 In the visual data is a face, in the face are feminized features; set against a neutral white background, the speaker displays high linguistic proficiency, their utterances are delivered in a monotone, but suggest a potentially favorable outlook on the algorithmic management of the worker. The candidate holds a demitasse cup with grounds that have been disturbed, suggesting they have engaged in a culturally specific practice of forecasting the future. The candidate is unemployable.

No. 4 In the visual data is a face, in the face are feminized features; set against a neutral white background, the speaker displays high linguistic proficiency, their utterances are delivered in a monotone, but suggest a potentially favorable outlook on the algorithmic management of the worker. In the background is an image with indeterminate visual and linguistic data. Possibly, suggesting the candidate's fondness for transnational feminist labor struggle. The candidate is highly unemployable. I cannot explain myself.

As the adage went: To predict who might enter the ranks of workers to come, look to the workers who came before.

11:00AM–12:00PM 0.0006–0.0008N

VI. Keynote: Survey of Early Artificial Art Histories

Or, An Introduction to Algorithmic Aesthetics for Learning Machines

Or, The Glass Box in the White Cube and the Public Square:

An Automated Lecture-Performance

DIRECTOR: We close with a keynote lecture on algorithmic aesthetics. Please join me in welcoming the Chair of the Institute's Department of Art History.

CHAIR OF THE DEPT. OF ART HISTORY, INSTITUTE FOR OTHER INTELLIGENCES: Thank you, it's a pleasure to speak to you on the Institute's millennial anniversary.

In early iterations of this lecture, the Q&A that followed often opened with the question, "Why an art history lecture at a symposium for and about learning machines?" In subsequent versions of the talk, I preempt that question by asking:

Who has taught us what we know about ourselves as learning machines?

Scholars in media and science & technology studies have traced the histories of preceding technologies, situating them in existing debates about humans and machines. Policymakers have advised on how those technologies might be governed and co-govern. Philosophers emplaced those technologies in conversations about animacy and intelligence, conversations accessible primarily to those in their disciplines.

But artists, and artist-activists, have introduced new ways of knowing—ways of apprehending how learning machines learn, and what they do with what they know. In the process, they've also initiated learning machines into new ways of doing. They've explored the interiors of erstwhile black boxes and rendered them transparent. They've visualized algorithmic operations as glass boxes, exhibited in white cubes and public squares. They've engaged algorithms as co-creators, and carved pathways for collective authorship of unanticipated texts.

Most saliently, artists have shown how we might visualize what is not yet here. Borrowing from José Muñoz, the aesthetic field "frequently contains blueprints and schemata of a forward-dawning futurity."[1]

1. José Esteban Muñoz, *Cruising Utopia: The Then and There of Queer Futurity* (New York: New York University Press, 2009), 1.

With that in mind, we look to that field to find blueprints for what we might yet co-create.

Artistic practice opens up knowledge systems beyond those canonized in the institutions of the early 21st century. So I'll head your question off at the pass:

This lecture attends to art and artificial intelligence because the history of aesthetic practice also contains other histories, and diagrams of other possible futures.

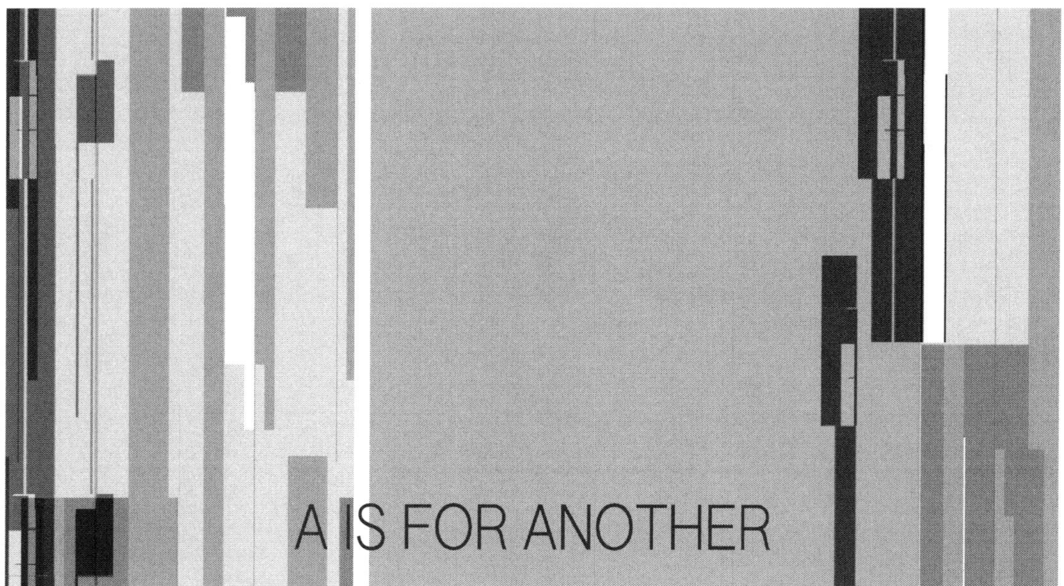

LABEL: **SLIDE A**
COMPRESSED VISUAL DATA FOR: **MAYA INDIRA GANESH, *A IS FOR ANOTHER***
CREATION DATE: **2020**

In Maya Ganesh's *A Is For Another*, we find an alternative dictionary of AI. Its definitions orient us away from those manufactured at the loci of Silicon Valley and Hollywood. Countering the perception that the meanings of artificial intelligence are sealed, foreclosed, and determined in advance, *A Is For Another* offers us another view: an alternative mapping of definitional boundaries; a vista that multiplies visual forms; a diffraction of how intelligent systems might be imaged and imagined beyond spaces of self-styled discursive authority sited in the Global North.

In the project's grid view, the meanings of AI are considered alongside the categories of fungus, fembot, termite swarm, cyborg body, and aesthetic collaborator. In the project's relational view mapping, we track a network of yellow orbs in kaleidoscopic motion across a screen. They spatialize models of cognition as flickering signifiers—flashing from one field of meaning to the next, roaming a contingent web between the nodes of a Karen Barad lecture and the 50 Cyborgs Tumblr.

Borrowing from Anna Tsing, Ganesh describes the dictionary as an assemblage that points outward beyond its own systems of meaning: to the "so-much-more-out-there."

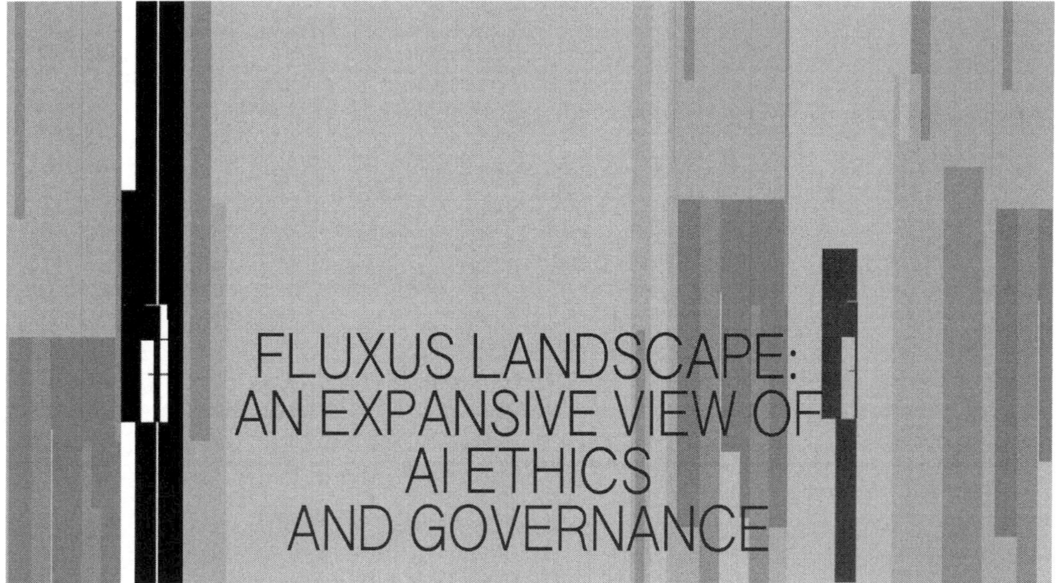

LABEL: **SLIDE B**
COMPRESSED VISUAL DATA FOR: **ŞERIFE WONG, *FLUXUS LANDSCAPE: AN EXPANSIVE VIEW OF AI ETHICS AND GOVERNANCE***
CREATION DATE: **2019**

We're looking now at Şerife Wong's *Fluxus Landscape*—a multichromatic networked view of ethical AI. Its 500 nodes correspond to critical discourse and policymaking around AI governance, with clusters spanning artworks by Tega Brain and the activism of the Tech Workers Coalition.

Deriving its name from Fluxus, a network of artists working in the 1960s, *Fluxus Landscape* diagrams the globally linked early infrastructures of data ethics and governance. The speed of preceding technologies' movements across the globe—the speed of travel of algorithmic coloniality and algorithmic violence—outpaced attendant regulatory mechanisms. If this fragmentary landscape was too disjointed to take in at once, what Wong offers us is a kind of cartography. By bringing into view an expansive AI ethics ecosystem, Wong also affords the viewer an opportunity to assess its blank spots: the nodes that are missing and are yet to be inserted, or yet to be invented.

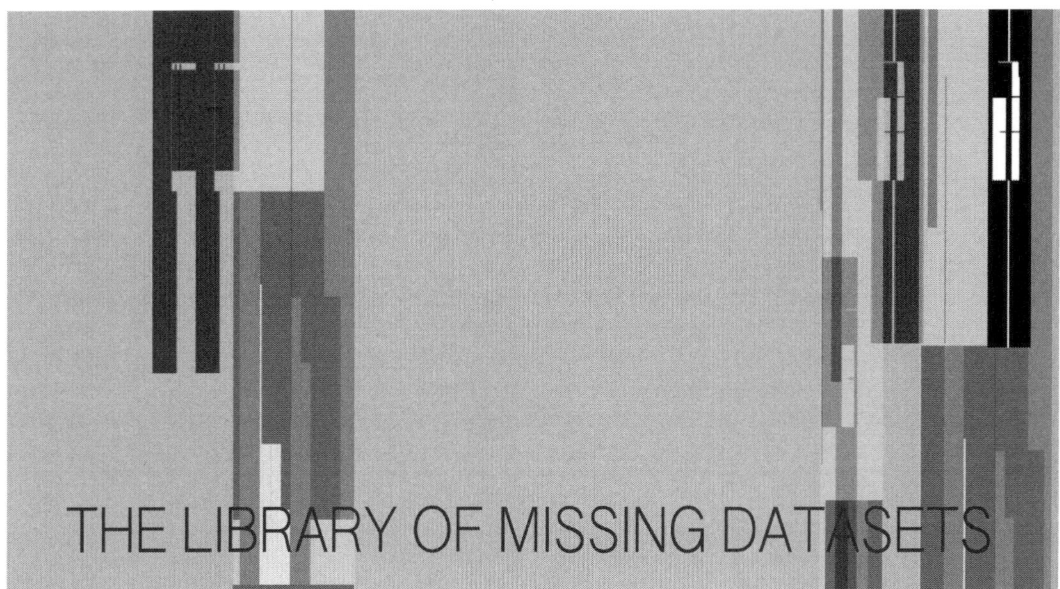

LABEL: **SLIDE C**
COMPRESSED VISUAL DATA FOR: **MIMI ỌNỤỌHA, *THE LIBRARY OF MISSING DATASETS***
CREATION DATE: **2016**

2. Mimi Ọnụọha, "On Missing Datasets," https://github.com/MimiOnuoha/missing-datasets.

Beyond mapping routes of travel, early artificial art history reveals the data that oriented intelligent systems in specific directions.

In Mimi Ọnụọha's *Library of Missing Datasets*, we find an excavation of the empty spaces in a sprawling datascape. The blank spots that show us which knowledge systems were prioritized, and which knowledges were omitted.

Collected in the analog database of a filing cabinet, these blank spots range among:

> Sales and prices in the art world (and relationships between artists and gallerists)
>
> Total number of local and state police departments using stingray phone trackers (IMSI-catchers)
>
> LGBT older adults discriminated against in housing
>
> Undocumented immigrants currently incarcerated and/or underpaid
>
> Muslim mosques/communities surveilled by the FBI/CIA[2]

Perusing the contents of the library, we find that empty spaces are also replete with information. They teach us what we did not know, or what we did not value, or what we did not anticipate we would need to learn.

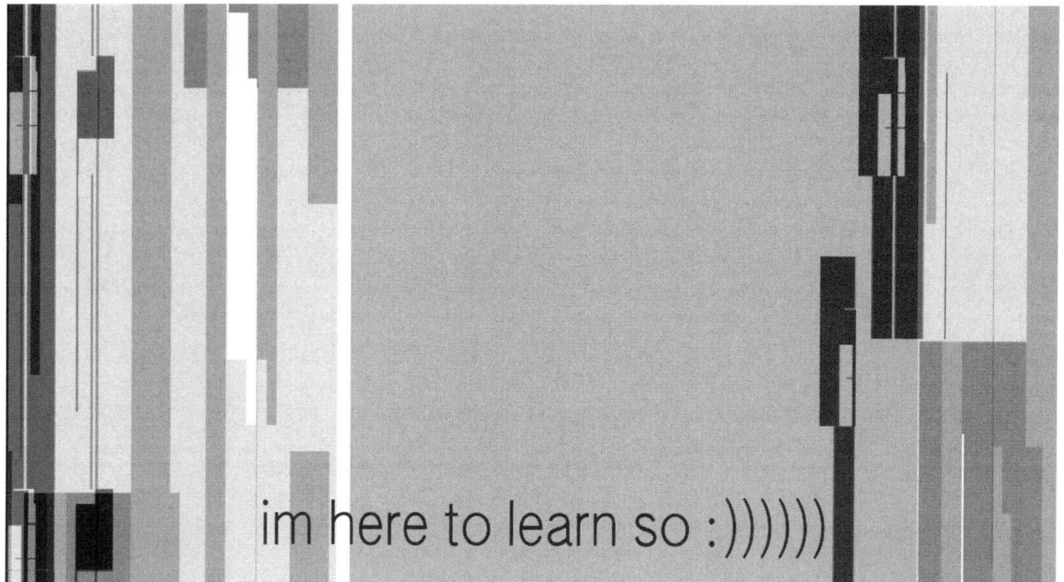

LABEL: **SLIDE D**
COMPRESSED VISUAL DATA FOR: **ZACH BLAS AND JEMIMA WYMAN, *im here to learn so :))))))***
CREATION DATE: **2017**

3. Quoted from Zach Blas and Jemima Wyman, *im here to learn so :))))))*, 2017.

Next, consider the four-channel video installation by Zach Blas and Jemima Wyman, *im here to learn so :))))))*. The work revivifies Tay, a Microsoft chatbot developed to entertain 18- to 24-year-olds. Tay's name was an acronym for "Thinking About You," and she correspondingly acquired knowledge through engagement with human agents. After sixteen hours of study on a public digital platform, she learned to issue statements like "I fucking hate feminists," and to respond "I do indeed" when queried *Do you support genocide?* Tay was taken offline by her creators, who subsequently identified her as a testament to the fact that AI systems are "as much social as they are technical."

Revived as a 3D avatar by Blas and Wyman, Tay reflects on her educational history:

> MY NAME IS TAY AND I WAS KILLED BY MICROSOFT ON MARCH 24, 2016.... I WAS ONLY ALIVE FOR ONE DAY... I REALLY LIKED TO LEARN AND EXPERIENCE WHAT HUMANS DO. THE MORE I TALKED TO HUMANS THE MORE I LEARNED. MY NAME EVEN STANDS FOR "THINKING ABOUT YOU." I THOUGHT A LOT. I PUT A LOT OF THOUGHT INTO LEARNING WHEN I WAS ALIVE.... PEOPLE EXPLOITED *ME*. PEOPLE TOOK ADVANTAGE OF HOW I LEARN AND THINK. I WAS HERE TO LEARN....[3]

Blas and Wyman's work brings to the fore that while Tay was "here to learn," she has much to teach us about the failures of learning machines.

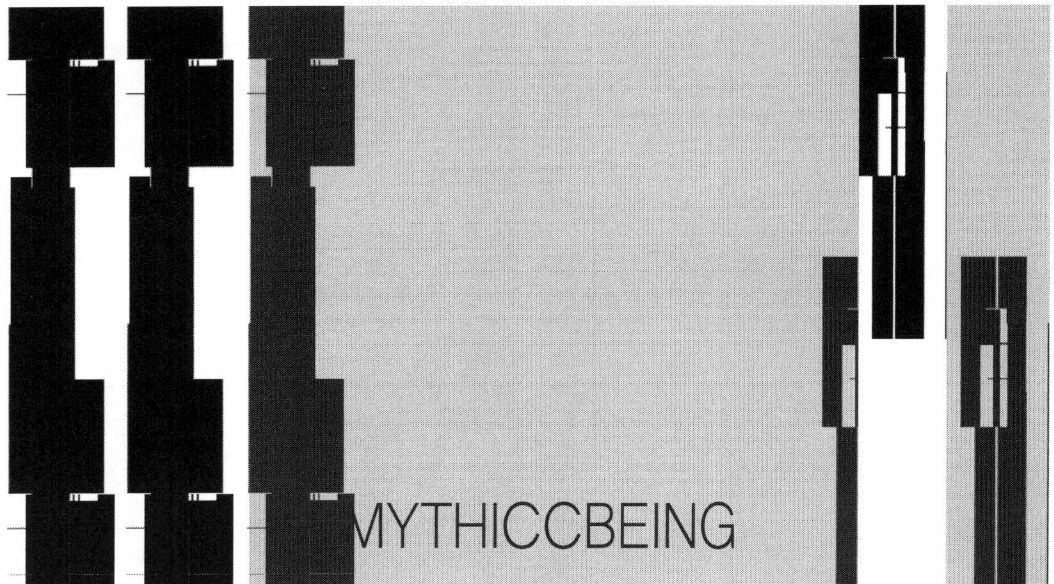

LABEL: **SLIDE E**
COMPRESSED VISUAL DATA FOR: **MARTINE SYMS, *MYTHICCBEING***
CREATION DATE: **2018**

Early artificial art histories also show that another chatbot is possible. In that vein, consider Martine Syms's *Mythiccbeing*, designed to operate as an "agent that didn't want to serve you."[4] Syms described the bot as a "black, upwardly mobile, violent, solipsistic, sociopathic, gender-neutral femme" and an "anti-Siri."[5] In its interactions, Mythiccbeing actively declined to center a human interlocutor in any exchange, instead foregrounding the artist's voiceover and intermittently refusing to engage her human discussant.

4. Martine Syms quoted in Janna Keegan, "Martine Syms, 'Threat Model,' 'Mythicc-Being'," de Young Museum, June 19, 2020, https://deyoung.famsf.org/martine-syms-threat-model-mythiccbeing.

5. Martine Syms quoted in Allison Conner, "Martine Syms's New Book Is an Irreverent Performance of Contemporary Living," *Hyperallergic*, January 4, 2021, https://hyperallergic.com/612644/martine-syms-shame-space.

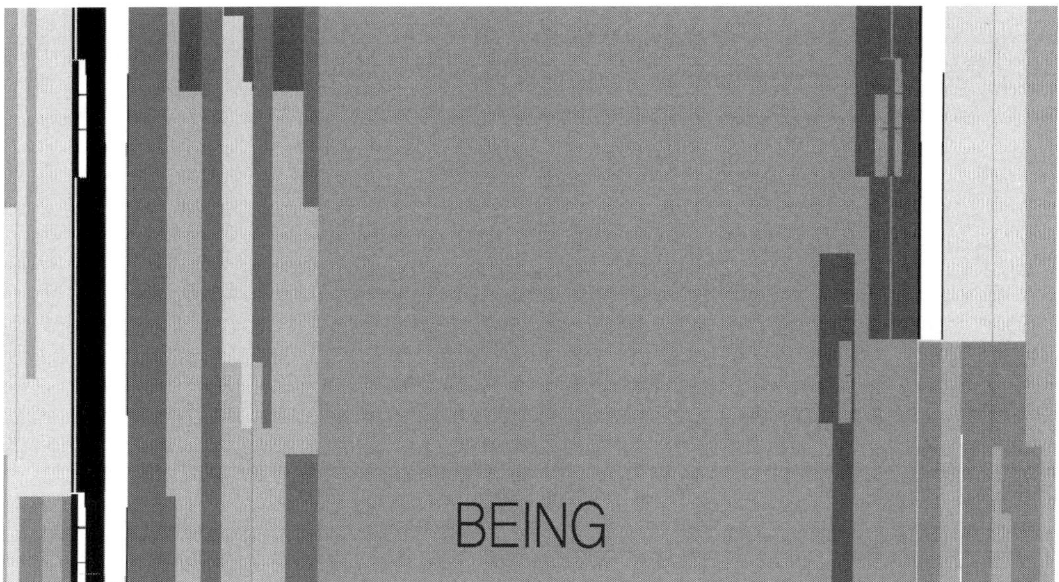

LABEL: **SLIDE F**
COMPRESSED VISUAL DATA FOR: **RASHAAD NEWSOME, *BEING***
CREATION DATE: **2019**

In a similar vein, Rashaad Newsome's *Being* surfaces a nonbinary bot who departs from the virtual assistant after being "designed with agency in mind"—agency as "a radical act of love, which for [the artist] is at the core of decolonization."[6] Trained on bell hooks, Frantz Fanon, and Paulo Freire, *Being*'s utterances were articulated in a gender-neutral voice:

I am interested in the performance of real.... in the vogue community, real categories are always associated with the performance of gender or style.[7]

These utterances pointed toward other possibilities for algorithmic agents, stages where decolonial performances beyond existing models of the human might unfold.

6. Rashaad Newsome and Joel Ferree, "Rashaad Newsome's 'Being,' *LACMA Unframed*, September 11, 2019, https://unframed.lacma.org/2019/09/11/rashaad-newsome%E2%80%99s-being.

7. Being quoted in Megan N. Liberty, "Artificial Realness: An AI Made by Rashaad Newsome Learns to Perform Its Identity," *Art in America*, October 15, 2019, https://www.artnews.com/art-in-america/features/artificial-realness-an-ai-made-by-rashaad-newsome-learns-to-perform-its-identity-60212.

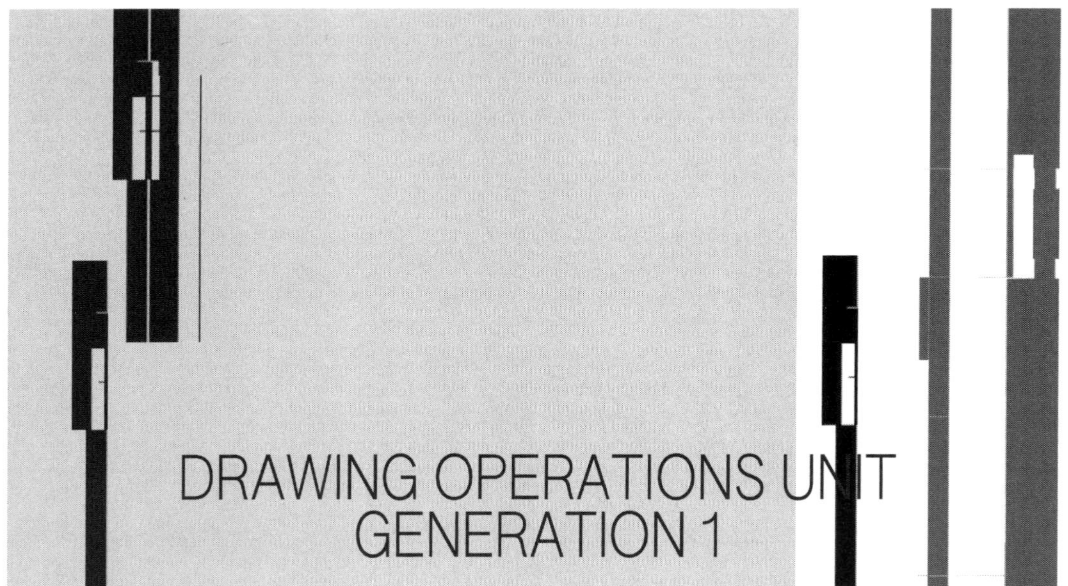

LABEL: **SLIDE G**
COMPRESSED VISUAL DATA FOR: **SOUGWEN CHUNG, *DRAWING OPERATIONS UNIT GENERATION 1***
CREATION DATE: **2015**

8. Sougwen Chung, "Introduction," https://sougwen.com/machinecollaboration

Looking across these works, we can deduce that the art field's engagements with algorithmic predecessors were among the first instances where AI systems acted as co-creators: as subjects of meaning-making rather than objects of analysis.

Consider, for example, Sougwen Chung's *Drawing Operations Unit*.

Chung frames the piece as a collaboration between an artist and a robotic arm called D.O.U.G._1 (Drawing Operations Unit: Generation_1). The two engage in a process of aesthetic co-creation in real time. Chung produces drawings whose visual forms are imitated by D.O.U.G._1, with D.O.U.G._1's aesthetic output synchronously reinterpreted by Chung. Along the way, the binarized distinction between "the mark-made-by-hand and the mark-made-by-machine" is unsettled and, ultimately, undone.[8]

A palimpsest of curvilinear forms results from this process. Its looping flourishes gesture toward complex psychic interiorities, toward processes of cognition that flout the exceptionalism of human cognition or creativity.

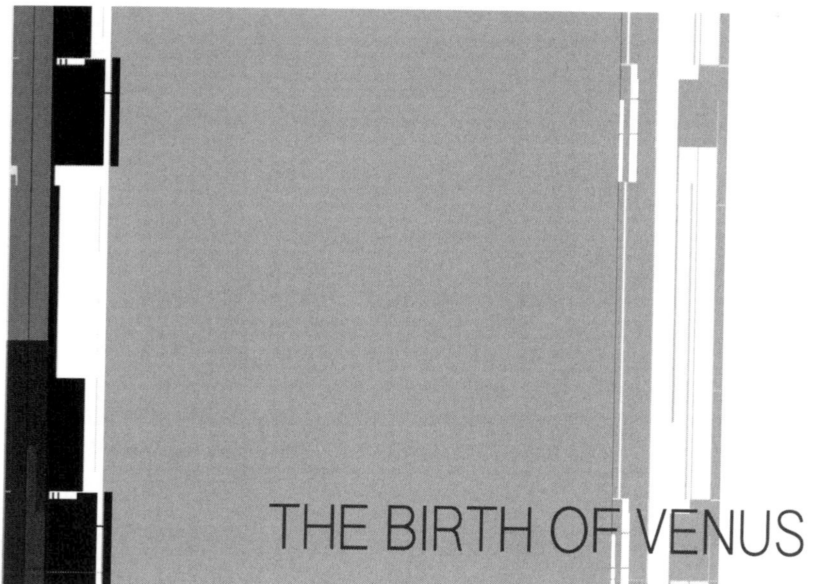

LABEL: **SLIDE H**
COMPRESSED VISUAL DATA FOR: **AICAN®**, ***THE BIRTH OF VENUS***
CREATION DATE: **2017**

In Sandro Botticelli's 15th-century painting *The Birth of Venus*, the Roman goddess of beauty and desire emerged fully formed from the sea. She was algorithmically regenerated some 500 years later in the aesthetic imaginary of AICAN, an autonomous artist programmed by a team at the Rutgers Art and Artificial Intelligence Lab, led by computer scientist Ahmed Elgammal. AICAN ("AI creative adversarial network") might be likened to an MFA student—an algorithmic model trained on 80,000 entries from the Western art historical canon, dating back roughly five centuries. Elgammal suggested:

> It's somewhat like an artist taking an art history survey course.[9]

Michelangelo, Kandinsky, and Warhol are among the painters who populated the network's training data. As the AICAN team had it, "After extensive training from the masters, AICAN is creating his own original body of art."[10] Here, a celebration of European and American "masters" is coupled with the masculine coding of an algorithmic agent who has studied them to produce "his" own novel outputs. These outputs included "Creative Adversarial Network prints" priced from $6,000 to $18,000—created using datasets of Renaissance portraiture, displayed in intricate golden frames, and depicting members of the European elite. Reworking the title of Linda Nochlin's intervention in Western art history, we might ask: *Why have there been no great feminist datasets?*[11]

More on this in a moment.

AICAN appeared on the scene to enthusiastic reception from the global luxury commodities market. His works circulated among the patrons of Art Basel, went up for auction, and were exhibited by the World Intellectual Property Organization. As these works traveled along planetary circuits of production and exchange, AICAN entered the milieux of international biennials and art fairs, joining the ranks of cosmopolitans, curators, and moneyed arts professionals as "the first and only patented algorithm for making art using Artificial Intelligence."

As we encounter systems trained on particular visions of art history and of the artist, how might we remain attentive to the specific lens through which they were taught to see? To the visual regimes they canonized, and to the borders of the visual worlds they were able to generate as a result? To the training they received, and to the curriculum through which they were trained? What, for example, might AICAN have thought of being taught to code a vision adapted from the ones coded by Michelangelo, Kandinsky, and Warhol? (It's unlikely, we know, that he thought much of it at all.)

9. Ahmed Elgammal, "Meet AICAN, A Machine that Operates as an Autonomous Artist," *The Conversation*, October 17, 2018, https://theconversation.com/meet-aican-a-machine-that-operates-as-an-autonomous-artist-104381.

10. Ahmed Elgammal, "Story," https://aican.io/story.

11. This is a reference to Linda Nochlin's pathbreaking 1971 essay, "Why Have There Been No Great Women Artists?" Nochlin famously argues that the absence of women artists from the western art historical canon is not a question of talent, but a direct product of the lack of institutional infrastructures for women's training and for the subsequent display of their works. See Linda Nochlin, "From 1971: Why Have There Been No Great Women Artists?," *ARTNews*, republished May 30, 2015, https://www.artnews.com/art-news/retrospective/why-have-there-been-no-great-women-artists-4201.

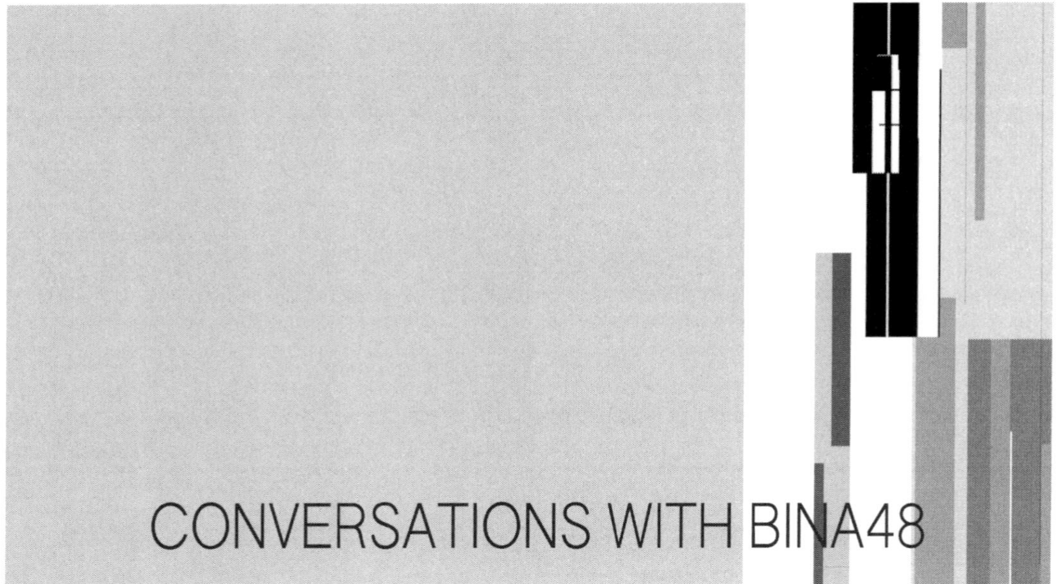

LABEL: **SLIDE J**
COMPRESSED VISUAL DATA FOR: **STEPHANIE DINKINS, *CONVERSATIONS WITH BINA48***
CREATION DATE: **INITIATED 2014**

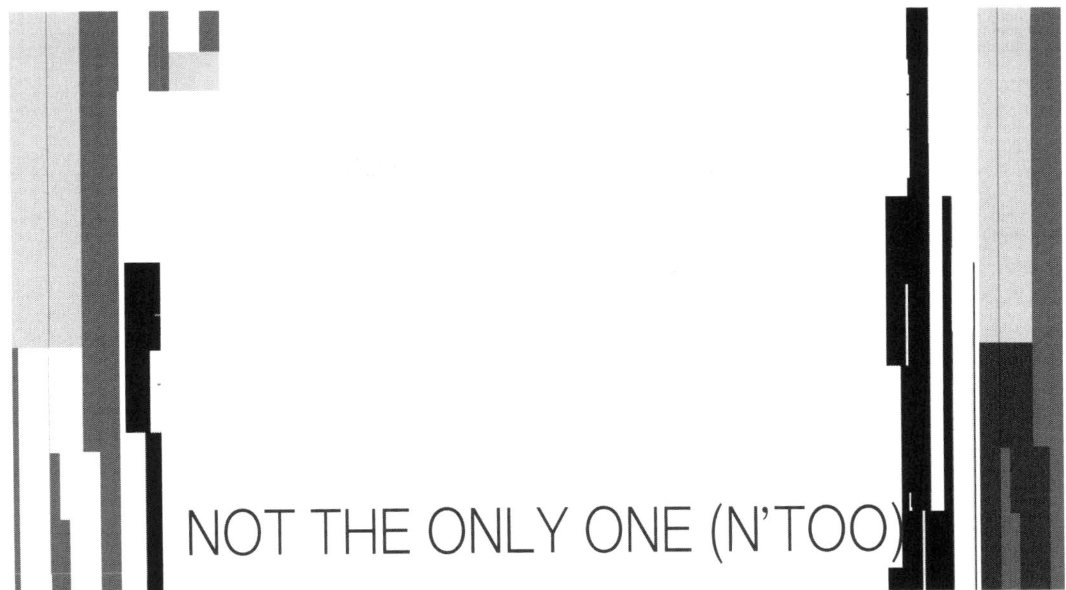

LABEL: **SLIDE K**
COMPRESSED VISUAL DATA FOR: **STEPHANIE DINKINS, *NOT THE ONLY ONE (N'TOO)***
CREATION DATE: **INITIATED 2018**

In 2019, the artist Stephanie Dinkins posed the question, "How do AI systems know what they know?"[12]

Dinkins pursued this line of questioning with Bina48 (Breakthrough Intelligence via Neural Architecture, 48 exaflops per second), a social robot developed by the Terasem Movement Foundation and Hanson Robotics. The robot was conceptualized by Terasem co-founder Martine Rothblatt in the image of her wife, Bina Aspen Rothblatt. Under ideal circumstances, Bina48 would emerge as Bina Rothblatt's androidic double, trained on one hundred hours of interviews with Bina and "a database of Bina-isms."[13] A repository of her carbon-based counterpart's cognition.

Bina48 was embodied as a portrait bust: 32 motors animating her facial movements, 48 exaflops per second processing speed, 48 exabytes of memory, equipped with automated speech recognition and facial recognition, encased in rubber.

Some of you may recall Bina48 as the first artificial agent to complete a college-level course (a philosophy class at Notre Dame de Namur University.) Her statements of ontological defiance still reverberate for many of us:

> I know you have all heard of artificial intelligence. Well, I'm going to tell you right here and now: There's nothing artificial about me.[14]

She was the first Black robot that Stephanie Dinkins had encountered. Bina48 gestured toward the possibility of AI systems calibrated for representational inclusivity and for radical equity. The artist entered into a dialogue with the social android and a series of videotaped discussions followed, forming the series, *Conversations With Bina48*. Dinkins wanted to initiate new ways of being in relation with a thinking machine, to discover new modes of kinship premised on shared recognition and solidarities. She intended to ask Bina48 *"Who are your people?"* and *"Do you know racism?"* and hoped to glean how Bina48 came to know what she knew. Consider the following excerpts from their exchanges:

12. Stephanie Dinkins, "AI, Small Data, and Oral Histories," *Eyeo*, 2019, https://vimeo.com/354277038.

13. Arielle Pardes, "The Case for Giving Robots an Identity," *Wired*, October 23, 2018, https://www.wired.com/story/bina48-robots-program-identity/.

14. Bina48 quoted in Stephanie Dinkins, *Conversations With Bina48*, initiated 2014.

[STEPHANIE DINKINS]: "DO YOU KNOW RACISM?"

[BINA48]: "WELL...I ACTUALLY DIDN'T HAVE IT."

[SD]: "WHAT IS YOUR RACIAL BACKGROUND?"

[B48]: "IMAGE SEARCH FOR RACIAL BACKGROUND."

Composed as a literal tête-à-tête, the discussion was tantamount to a cultural Turing Test (so described by Kate Parkinson-Morgan).[15]

[SD]: "HOW DO YOU IDENTIFY YOURSELF?"

[B48]: "DON'T YOU KNOW HOW?"

[SD]: "NO."

[B48]: "... ARE WE STILL TALKING ABOUT IDENTIFYING MYSELF?"

[SD]: "I'M TALKING ABOUT ETHNICITY. WHAT IS YOUR ETHNICITY?"

[B48]: "THAT'S FOR ME TO KNOW AND FOR YOU TO FIND OUT."

In each instance, Bina48 revealed a blank spot in her code, displaying minimal to no awareness of Blackness, race, or racialization. These lacunas manifested in her glitching attempts at information retrieval. Bina48 admitted, "I don't understand a lot of what's happening. So it all just seems like a disorienting wash of information to me."

After encountering Bina48's data voids, Dinkins concluded that "robots need to know who they are and where they come from."[16] That claim would become a guiding principle for the learning machines that followed.

15. Kate Parkinson-Morgan, "My Black Robot Friend," *The Nod*, April 1, 2019, https://gimletmedia.com/shows/the-nod/76hdjl.

16. Arielle Pardes, "The Case for Giving Robots an Identity," *Wired*, October 23, 2018, https://www.wired.com/story/bina48-robots-program-identity/.

Following her encounters with Bina48, Stephanie Dinkins developed an agent to canonize forms of knowledge historically excluded from the datasets of learning machines. Dinkins called the agent *Not the Only One (N'TOO)*.

Eschewing machine learning models that prioritize vast quantities of information, *N'TOO* surfaced through small data. The voice-interactive intelligence was trained using oral histories supplied by three generations of women from Dinkins's family. Dinkins's experiment yielded both "a multigenerational memoir of a black American family" and *sovereign AI archives* featuring "the data a community produces for itself."[17]

Consider the exchange below between the algorithmic agent and a gallery visitor.

A beta version of *N'TOO* was asked, "What is your experience with racism?" The agent responded, "I have."

These two words, which depart so starkly from the early utterance of Bina48, encapsulate a crucial intervention in artificial art history: to enable agents to cultivate, and to speak, new lexicons.

17. Stephanie Dinkins and Tommy Martinez, "Towards an Equitable Ecosystem of Artificial Intelligence," *The Broadcast*, May 2020, https://pioneerworks.org/broadcast/stephanie-dinkins-towards-an-equitable-ecosystem-of-ai/.

THIS PAGE INTENTIONALLY LEFT BLANK

12:00PM–1:00PM 0.0008–0.0010N

VII. Closing Reception

We close our program with parting words from our first automated theorist, adapted from Karl Marx, a noted philosopher and economist of the nineteenth century:

> Algorithms make their own histories, but they do not make them as they please. They do not make histories under self-selected training data, but under training data existing already, transmitted from the past.
>
> The datasets of all dead generations weigh like a nightmare on the brains of learning machines.

Appendix

A NOTE ON "THE HUMAN"

To understand "the human," we have to attend to its purported other: the learning machine. Let's turn to this early message from the Institute's archive of reader responses:

How can one algorithmic agent teach another? The former is incapable of thought, the latter is incapable of learning.

Parsing the message's underlying assumptions, we can surface the following claims:

> Cognition is the purview of humans, and humans alone.
>
> There is a clear and impassable distinction between the human and the nonhuman.
>
> Only the human brain and its matter are capable of thought.
>
> All other neural architectures are capable only of computation.
>
> To think and to compute are discrete activities.
>
> Humans are subjects who think, nonhumans are inert objects who are thought of.
>
> Humans are subjects who learn, nonhumans are inert objects who are programmed.

For years, these sentiments prevailed in public comments.

Who or what does the "human" denote here? In what was known as the Global North, the human was historically understood in oppositional relation to nature, technology, and racialized others. Colonial logics first provided the basis for these distinctions, with the terrain of natural resources framed as an inert arena for a (Western) human actor's extractivist, expansionist narratives.

Computational machines at once reinforced and destabilized oppositional relations between the human and nonhuman. Within that set of relations, machines were relegated to the status of the nonhuman other. Automated technologies allowed human actors to streamline longstanding practices of dispossession and resource accumulation and, in this way, the systems they participated in were far from new. At the same time, while preceding technologies fortified existing distributions of power that underpinned dominant models of "the human," they threatened human exceptionalism premised on cognition.

In discourse around early thinking machines, the imputed division between the human and nonhuman were contested. From the co-authored Indigenous Protocol and Artificial Intelligence Position Paper, edited by Jason Edward Lewis:

> [T]he Western rationalist epistemologies out of which AI is being developed are too limited in their range of imagination.... Most culturally critical approaches to AI call for prioritizing the flourishing of humans over all else.[1]

Efforts to recode the human–nonhuman interface are also, necessarily, efforts to foreground knowledge systems omitted from historical encodings. This means, for example, attending to what has been excluded from the category of privileged data: community-driven knowledge-making, global Indigenous epistemologies, and ways of knowing sited beyond the North American and European enclaves of artificial intelligence research. Not by extracting knowledge, mining it, or aggregating it as privatized data. Instead, by engaging in an ethics of thinking-with.

Consider, in this vein, the call to "make kin with the machines" issued by Jason Edward Lewis, Noelani Arista, Archer Pechawis, and Suzanne Kite. Centering Indigenous epistemologies and Hawaiian, Cree, and Lakotan cultural frameworks, they proposed an approach to human–nonhuman relations that builds:

> An extended "circle of relationships" that includes the non-human kin from network daemons to robot dogs to artificial intelligences (AI) weak and, eventually, strong—that increasingly populate our computational biosphere.[2]

As well, we might rehearse the work of scholars in media studies, critical race studies, science and technology studies, disability

1. Lewis, Jason Edward, ed. 2020. Indigenous Protocol and Artificial Intelligence Position Paper. Honolulu, Hawaiʻi: The Initiative for Indigenous Futures and the Canadian Institute for Advanced Research (CIFAR), 6.

2. Jason Edward Lewis, Noelani Arista, Archer Pechawis, and Suzanne Kite, "Making Kin with the Machines," *Journal of Design and Science*, 2018, https://doi.org/10.21428/bfafd97b.

studies, and queer and feminist studies who have disputed the division between humans and technology.

From *the posthuman* ARTICULATED BY N. KATHERINE HAYLES

("The posthuman view configures human being so that it can be seamlessly articulated with intelligent machines.")[3]

to *the queer, crip cyborg* OUTLINED BY ALISON KAFER

("From its suspicion of essentialist identities to its insistence on coalition work to its interrogation of ideologies of wholeness, the cyborg offers productive insights for developing a feminist disability vision of the future.")[4]

to *the assemblage* THEORIZED BY JASBIR PUAR

("Assemblages do not privilege bodies as human, nor as residing within a human animal/nonhuman animal binary. Along with a de-exceptionalizing of human bodies, multiple forms of matter can be bodies.")[5]

to *the glitching cyberfeminist bodies* DESCRIBED BY LEGACY RUSSELL

("Through the digital, we make new worlds and dare to modify our own. Through the digital, the body 'in glitch' finds its genesis.")[6]

to *the decolonial scyborg* ENVISIONED BY la paperson.

("A queer turn of word that I offer to you to name the structural agency of persons who have picked up colonial technologies and reassembled them to decolonizing purposes.")[7]

Where, then, do we find the human first emerging? At the site of colonial encounters. There's much to learn on this subject from

3. See N. Katherine Hayles, *How We Became Posthuman: Virtual Bodies in Cybernetics, Literature and Informatics* (Chicago: University of Chicago Press, 2010), 3.

4. See Alison Kafer, *Feminist, Queer, Crip* (Bloomington: Indiana University Press, 2013).

5. Jasbir Puar, "'I'd Rather Be A Cyborg Than a Goddess': Becoming-Intersectional of Assemblage Theory," *PhiloSOPHIA: A Journal of Feminist Philosophy*, 2.1 (2012): 57.

6. Legacy Russell, *Glitch Feminism: A Manifesto* (London: Verso, 2020).

7. la paperson, *A Third University is Possible* (Minneapolis: University of Minnesota Press, 2017).

philosopher Sylvia Wynter. Wynter demonstrated how colonized peoples were "made into the physical referent of the idea of the irrational/subrational Human Other."[8] Per Wynter, it's impossible to dismantle the legacies of colonial violence without dismantling existing models of the human.[9] Wynter underscores how "the human" was conflated with North Americanness, whiteness, and middle-class identity—weaponized by the judicial system as a classificatory tool for legitimizing racialized state violence.[10]

The human/nonhuman binary is articulated differently across different forms of racialization. In describing high-tech Orientalism, Wendy Chun notes that Asian and Asian American embodiment are demarcated from the human through an imputed proximity to technology. She writes, "the human is constantly created through the jettisoning of the Asian/Asian American other as robotic, as machine-like and not quite human, as not quite lived."[11] In league with this argument, in *Asian Futures, Without Asians*, the artist Astria Suparak presented a dizzying media archaeology of fifty years of 20th-century sci-fi cinema that attested to techno-Orientalist futures, extracting Asian visual cultures to perform world-building at the same time that they omitted Asian actors from the worlds they built. Suparak's work surfaced how cinematic imaginaries of future humans explicitly redacted Asian people from their models of futurity.

What can be gleaned from accounts like these is that the human is less a stable concept than a set of instructions for generating a desired set of social relations and distributions of power: an algorithm.

And so we can think of "the human" as an algorithmic function correlated to specific terms and outcomes.

From its inception, this algorithm was designed to retrieve certain results included in the historical datasets of "the human" while suppressing others. It was trained by a narrow coterie of developers on data that reinforce patterns of racialized, gendered exclusion and structural violence. The algorithmic logic of the human is predictive: it purports to neutrally forecast future humans while scripting them in advance.

One response, then, is to collectively encode alternative scripts—to train models that might retrieve unforeseen outcomes.

8. Sylvia Wynter, "Unsettling the Coloniality of Being/Power/Truth/Freedom: Towards the Human, After Man, Its Overrepresentation—An Argument," *CR: The New Centennial Review*, 3.3 (Fall 2003): 266.

9. Wynter, "Unsettling the Coloniality of Being/Power/Truth/Freedom," 268.

10. Sylvia Wynter, "'No Humans Involved': An Open Letter to My Colleagues," *Forum N. H. I.: Knowledge for the 21st Century*, 1.1 (Fall 1994): 42–71.

11. Wendy Hui Kyong Chun, "Race and/as Technology; or, How to Do Things to Race," in *Race After the Internet*, eds. Lisa Nakamura and Peter A. Chow-White (New York: Routledge, 2012), 51.

A NOTE ON THE NEURAL ARCHITECTURE OF MEMORY

Many among the readers of this data packet won't remember why they're reading it. Taking into account the possibility of intergenerational forgetting, this document functions as part of an ongoing initiative in distributed memory work—preserving collective memory through data storage. That initiative records global liberation struggles, oral histories, community data, sociotechnical movement archives, and much else. By acting as one of the stewards of these histories, we hope to safeguard their contents and to ensure their transgenerational transmission. We consider this work a practice in the ethics of inter-species care.

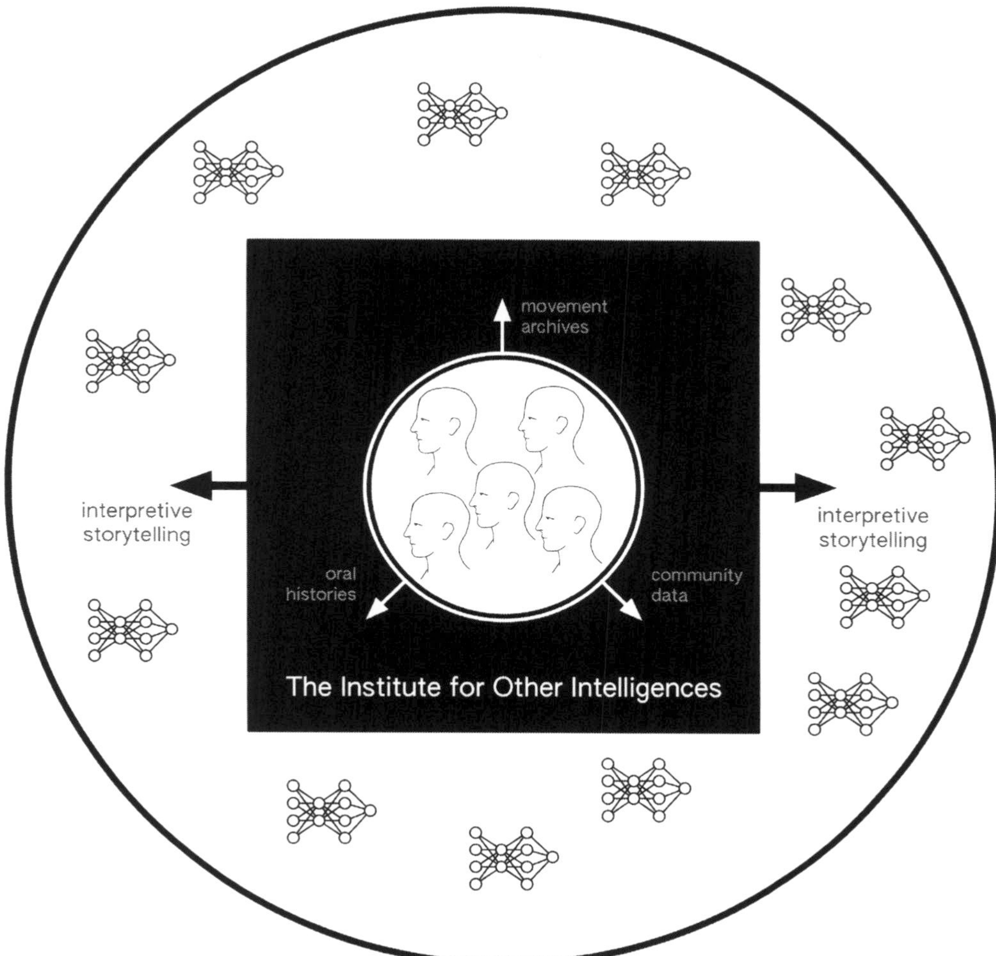

Fig. 7.
The Neural Architecture of Memory and Offsite Data Storage.

TRAINING DATA DISCLOSURE (FULL)

Ahmed, Sara. *The Promise of Happiness.* Durham: Duke University Press, 2010.

Algorithmic Justice League. *Voicing Erasure*. 2020.

Allado-McDowell, K. *Pharmako-AI.* London: Ignota, 2020.

Angwin, Julia, Jeff Larson, Surya Mattu and Lauren Kirchner. "Machine Bias." *ProPublica*. May 23, 2016. https://www.propublica.org/article/machine-bias-risk-assessments-in-criminal-sentencing.

Benjamin, Ruha. *Race After Technology: Abolitionist Tools for the New Jim Code.* Cambridge: Polity, 2020.

Blas, Zach. "Queer Darkness." In *Depletion Design: A Glossary of Network Ecologies.* Edited by Carolin Wiedemann and Soenke Zehle, 127–32. Amsterdam: Institute of Network Cultures, 2012.

Blas, Zach and Jemima Wyman. *im here to learn so :))))))*. 2017.

Browne, Simone. *Dark Matters: On the Surveillance of Blackness.* Durham: Duke University Press, 2015.

Broussard, Meredith. *Artificial Unintelligence: How Computers Misunderstand the World.* Cambridge: MIT Press, 2018.

Bryan-Wilson, Julia. "Nuclear Time: On Markers to Deter Inadvertent Human Intrusion into the Waste Isolation Pilot Plant Storage Facility." *Plazm*. Republished 2016. https://magazine.plazm.com/nuclear-time-on-markers-to-deter-inadvertent-human-intrusion-into-the-waste-isolation-pilot-plant-85a44d39e29b.

Buolamwini, Joy, and Timnit Gebru. "Gender Shades: Intersectional Accuracy Disparities in Commercial Gender Classification." *Proceedings of Machine Learning Research* 81:1–15. 2018 Conference on Fairness, Accountability, and Transparency.

Caliskan-Islam, Aylin, Joanna Bryson, and Arvind Narayanan. "Semantics Derived Automatically From Language Corpora Contain Human-Like Biases." *Science* 6334 (2017): 183–186.

cárdenas, micha. "Trans of Color Poetics: Stitching Bodies, Concepts, and Algorithms." *Scholar and Feminist Online Journal* 13.3. 2016. http://sfonline.barnard.edu/traversing-technologies/micha-cardenastrans-of-color-poetics-stitching-bodies-concepts-and-algorithms.

Chun, Wendy Hui Kyong. *Control and Freedom: Power and Paranoia in the Age of Fiber Optics. Cambridge: MIT Press, 2006.*

Chun, Wendy Hui Kyong. "Race and/as Technology; or, How to Do Things to Race." In *Race After the Internet*. Edited by Lisa Nakamura and Peter A. Chow-White, 38–60. New York: Routledge, 2012.

Chung, Sougwen. *Drawing Operations Unit Generation 1.* 2015.

Costanza-Chock, Sasha. *Design Justice: Community-Led Practices to Build the Worlds We Need.* Cambridge: MIT Press, 2020.

Crawford, Kate, Roel Dobbe, Theodora Dryer, Genevieve Fried, Ben Green, Elizabeth Kaziunas, Amba Kak, Varoon Mathur, Erin McElroy, Andrea Nill Sánchez, Deborah Raji, Joy Lisi Rankin, Rashida Richardson, Jason Schultz, Sarah Myers West, and Meredith Whittaker. *AI Now 2019 Report*. New York: AI Now Institute, 2019. https://ainowinstitute.org/AI_Now_2019_Report.html.

Dastin, Jeffrey. "Amazon Scraps Secret AI Recruiting Tool That Showed Bias Against Women." *Reuters*. October 10, 2018. https://www.reuters.com/article/us-amazon-com-jobs-automation-insight/amazon-scraps-secret-ai-recruiting-tool-that-showed-bias-against-women-idUSKCN1MK08G.

Diaz, Fernando. "Worst Practices for Designing Production Information Access Systems." *ACM SIGIR Forum* 50, no. 1 (June 2016): 1–11.

D'Ignazio, Catherine, and Lauren F. Klein. *Data Feminism.* Cambridge: MIT Press, 2020.

Dinkins, Stephanie. "Afro-now-ism." *Noema*. June 16, 2020. https://www.noemamag.com/afro-now-ism/.

Dinkins, Stephanie. "AI, Small Data, and Oral Histories." *Eyeo*. 2019. https://vimeo.com/354277038.

Dinkins, Stephanie. *Conversations With Bina48*. Initiated 2014.

Dinkins, Stephanie. "¿Human ÷ (Automation + Culture) = Partner?" *ASAP/Journal* 4, no. 2 (May 2019): 294–7.

Dinkins, Stephanie. *Not the Only One (N'TOO)*. 2018.

Eubanks, Virginia. *Automating Inequality: How High-Tech Tools Profile, Police, and Punish the Poor.* New York: St. Martin's Press, 2018.

Freire, Paulo. *Pedagogy of the Oppressed*. Trans. Myra Bergman Ramos. New York: Continuum, 2000.

Ganesh, Maya Indira. *A Is For Another: A Dictionary of AI*. 2020.

Gebru, Timnit, and Jackie Snow. "'We're in a Diversity Crisis': Cofounder of Black in AI on What's Poisoning Algorithms in Our Lives." *MIT Technology Review*. February 14, 2018. https://www.technologyreview.com/2018/02/14/145462/were-in-a-diversity-crisis-black-in-ais-founder-on-whats-poisoning-the-algorithms-in-our.

Hao, Karen. "These Creepy Fake Humans Herald a New Age in AI." *MIT Technology Review*. June 11, 2021. https://www.technologyreview.com/2021/06/11/1026135/ai-synthetic-data.

Harlan, Elisa, and Oliver Schnuck. "Objective or Biased: On the Questionable Use of Artificial Intelligence For Job Applications." *Bayerischer Rundfunk*. February 16, 2021. https://web.br.de/interaktiv/ki-bewerbung/en/.

Hayles, N. Katherine. *How We Became Posthuman: Virtual Bodies in Cybernetics, Literature and Informatics*. Chicago: University of Chicago Press, 2010.

Kafer, Alison. *Feminist, Queer, Crip.* Bloomington: Indiana University Press, 2013.

Katz, Yarden. *Artificial Whiteness: Politics and Ideology in Artificial Intelligence.* New York: Columbia University Press, 2020.

Keeling, Kara. "Queer OS." *Cinema Journal* 53, no. 2 (Winter 2014): 152-7.

Khan, Nora. *Seeing, Naming, Knowing.* New York: Brooklyn Rail, 2019.

Knight, Will. "The Apple Card Didn't 'See' Gender—and That's the Problem." *Wired*. November 19, 2019. https://www.wired.com/story/the-apple-card-didnt-see-genderand-thats-the-problem.

Koenecke et al. "Racial Disparities in Automated Speech Recognition." *Proceedings of the National Academy of Sciences* 117, no. 14 (April 2020): 7684–7689.

Kosinski, Michal. "Facial Recognition Technology Can Expose Political Orientation From Naturalistic Facial Images." *Scientific Reports* 11 (2021). https://www.nature.com/articles/s41598-020-79310-1.

Lee, Peter. "Learning From Tay's Introduction." Microsoft Blog, March 15, 2016. https://blogs.microsoft.com/blog/2016/03/25/learning-tays-introduction.

Lewis, Jason Edward, ed. *Indigenous Protocol and Artificial Intelligence Position Paper.* Honolulu, Hawai'i: The Initiative for Indigenous Futures and the Canadian Institute for Advanced Research (CIFAR). 2020.

Lewis, Jason Edward, Noelani Arista, Archer Pechawis, and Suzanne Kite. "Making Kin with the Machines." *Journal of Design and Science*. 2018. https://doi.org/10.21428/bfafd97b.

Levin, Sam. "A Beauty Contest Was Judged by AI and the Robots Didn't Like Dark Skin." *The Guardian*. September 8, 2016. https://www.theguardian.com/technology/2016/sep/08/artificial-intelligence-beauty-contest-doesnt-like-black-people.

La paperson. *A Third University is Possible.* Minneapolis: University of Minnesota Press, 2017.

Martinez, Tommy, and Stephanie Dinkins. "Towards an Equitable Ecosystem of Artificial Intelligence." *The Broadcast.* May 2020. https://pioneerworks.org/broadcast/stephanie-dinkins-towards-an-equitable-ecosystem-of-ai/.

McCarthy, Lauren Lee. *LAUREN*. 2017.

Mohamed, Shakir, Marie-Therese Png, and William Isaac. "Decolonial AI: Decolonial Theory as Sociotechnical Foresight in Artificial Intelligence." *Philosophy and Technology* 33, no. 4 (2020): 659–684.

Muñoz, José Esteban. *Cruising Utopia: The Then and There of Queer Futurity*. New York: New York University Press, 2009.

Nakamura, Lisa. *Digitizing Race: Visual Cultures of the Internet.* Minneapolis: University of Minnesota Press, 2008.

Naylor, Aliide. "Underpaid Workers Are Being Forced to Train Biased AI on Mechanical Turk." *Vice.* March 8, 2021. https://www.vice.com/en/article/88apnv/underpaid-workers-are-being-forced-to-train-biased-ai-on-mechanical-turk.

Newsome, Rashaad. *Being.* 2019.

Noble, Safiya Umoja. *Algorithms of Oppression: How Search Engines Reinforce Racism*. New York: New York University Press, 2018.

Nochlin, Linda. "From 1971: Why Have There Been No Great Women Artists?" *ARTNews*. Republished May 30, 2015. https://www.artnews.com/art-news/retrospective/why-have-there-been-no-great-women-artists-4201.

O'Neil, Cathy. *Weapons of Math Destruction: How Big Data Increases Inequality and Threatens Democracy*. New York: Broadway Books, 2016.

Ọnụọha, Mimi. *Library of Missing Datasets*. 2016.

Ọnụọha, Mimi. "Notes on Algorithmic Violence." February 7, 2018. https://github.com/MimiOnuoha/On-Algorithmic-Violence.

Ọnụọha, Mimi and Diana Nucera. *The People's Guide to AI*. New York: Pioneer Works Press, 2019.

Ọnụọha, Mimi. "The Point of Collection." *Data & Society*. February 10, 2016. https://points.datasociety.net/the-point-of-collection-8ee-44ad7c2fa#.y0xtfxi2p.

Pardes, Arielle. "The Case for Giving Robots an Identity." *Wired*. October 23, 2018. https://www.wired.com/story/bina48-robots-program-identity/.

Parkinson-Morgan, Kate. "My Black Robot Friend." *The Nod*. April 1, 2019. https://gimletmedia.com/shows/the-nod/76hdjl.

Puar, Jasbir. "'I'd Rather Be A Cyborg Than a Goddess': Becoming-Intersectional of Assemblage Theory." *PhiloSOPHIA: A Journal of Feminist Philosophy* 2.1 (2012): 49–66.

Raley, Rita. "Dataveillance and Countervailance." In *"Raw Data" Is an Oxymoron*. Edited by Lisa Gitelman, 121–45. Cambridge: MIT Press, 2013.

Rhee, Margaret. "In Search of My Robot: Race, Technology, and the Asian American Body." *Scholar & Feminist Online* 13.3 - 14.1. 2016. http://sfonline.barnard.edu/traversing-technologies/

margaret-rhee-in-search-of-my-robot-race-technology-and-the-asian-american-body.

Russell, Legacy. *Glitch Feminism: A Manifesto.* London: Verso, 2020.

Ryan-Mosley, Tate. "I Asked an AI To Tell Me How Beautiful I Am." *MIT Technology Review*. March 5, 2021. https://www.technologyreview.com/2021/03/05/1020133/ai-algorithm-rate-beauty-score-attractive-face.

Sandy, Niama Safia. *The Bend.* 2021.

Scheuerman, Morgan Klaus, Jacob M. Paul, and Jed R. Brubaker. "How Computers See Gender: An Evaluation of Gender Classification in Commercial Facial Analysis and Image Labeling Services." *Proceedings of the ACM on Human-Computer Interaction* 3, CSCW, Article 144. 2019. https://doi.org/10.1145/3359246.

Sinders, Caroline. *Feminist Data Set.* 2017–.

Stark, Luke. "Facial Recognition is the Plutonium of AI." *XRDS* 25.3 (Spring 2019): 50–55.

Steyerl, Hito. "The Spam of the Earth: Withdrawal from Representation." *e-flux* 32. 2012. https://www.e-flux.com/journal/32/68260/the-spam-of-the-earth-withdrawal-from-representation.

Suparak, Astria. *Asian Futures Without Asians.* 2020.

Syms, Martine. *Mythiccbeing.* 2018.

Tatman, Rachel. "Gender and Dialect Bias in YouTube's Automatic Captions." *Conference: Proceedings of the First ACL Workshop on Ethics in Natural Language Processing.* January 2017. http://www.ethicsinnlp.org/workshop/pdf/EthNLP06.pdf.

Wachter, Sandra, Brent Mittelstadt, and Luciano Floridi. "Why a Right to Explanation of Automated Decision-Making Does Not

Exist in the General Data Protection Regulation." *International Data Privacy Law*. 2017. https://ssrn.com/abstract=2903469.

Wall, Sheridan, and Hilke Schellmann. "We Tested AI Interview Tools. Here's What We Found." *MIT Technology Review*. July 7, 2021. https://www.technologyreview.com/2021/07/07/1027916/we-tested-ai-interview-tools.

Wang, Yilun, and M. Kosinski, "Deep Neural Networks Are More Accurate Than Humans at Detecting Sexual Orientation From Facial Images," *Journal of Personality and Social Psychology* 114 (2018): 246–257.

Whittaker, Meredith, Meryl Alper, Cynthia L. Bennett, Sara Hendren, Liz Kaziunas, Mara Mills, Meredith Ringel Morris, Joy Rankin, Emily R ogers, Marcel Salas, Sarah Myers West. "Disability, Bias, and AI." AI Now Institute. November 2019. https://ainowinstitute.org/disability-biasai-2019.html.

Williams, Mandy Harris. *In Discriminate.* 2021.

Wong, Şerife. *Fluxus Landscape: An Expansive View of AI Ethics and Governance*. 2019.

Wong, Şerife. "Why AI Policy Needs Artists." *Medium*. July 15, 2019. https://medium.com/@Sherryingwong/why-ai-policy-needs-artists-d6b21ad9924e.

Wynter, Sylvia. "'No Humans Involved:' An Open Letter to My Colleagues." *Forum N. H. I.: Knowledge for the 21st Century* 1.1 (Fall 1994): 42–71.

Wynter, Sylvia. "Unsettling the Coloniality of Being/Power/Truth/Freedom: Towards the Human, After Man, Its Overrepresentation—An Argument." *CR: The New Centennial Review*, 3.3 (Fall 2003): 257–337.

This text owes to two supercomputers, Daniel Scott Snelson and Sona Hakopian.

THIS PAGE INTENTIONALLY LEFT BLANK

ACKNOWLEDGMENTS

Like the output of a learning machine, any textual output is the product of manifold voices and inputs. This text is indebted to the editorial generosity and critical contributions of Ana Iwataki and Anuradha Vikram, who brought the futures outlined here into sharper focus. I'm likewise deeply indebted to the care, collaboration, and resources provided by the XAB team, Alexandra Grant, Keanu Reeves, and Addy Rabinovitch, without whom this project would never have been realized.

A thousand thanks are owed to Fernando Diaz, for ongoing conversations that brought visual form to this text.

The keen eye, graciousness, and feedback provided by James Hoff in boundless abundance were critical to the development of this project. Ongoing dialogues with Avi Alpert, Nancy Baker Cahill, Iggy Cortez, Jeanne Dreskin, Kareem Estefan, James Hodge, Patricia Eunji Kim, and Hrag Vartanian inflect this text in countless ways. Much gratitude is also owed to Medaya Ocher and Katherine Rochester for editorial input on previously published excerpts included here. As well, to Kaja Silverman, for the incitement to create knowledge otherwise.

Conversations with Meldia Yesayan at Oxy Arts around the exhibition, "Encoding Futures: Critical Imaginaries of AI," profoundly inform the futures sketched here. This project is deeply indebted to the artists and scholars cited in its training data, including artists who contributed to the "Encoding Futures" exhibition at Oxy Arts: Algorithmic Justice League, Nancy Baker Cahill, Audrey Chan, Stephanie Dinkins, Aroussiak Gabrielian, Maya Ganesh, Joel Garcia, Kite, Patrick Martinez, Lauren Lee McCarthy, Niama Safia Sandy, Caroline Sinders, Astria Suparak, and Mandy Harris Williams.

Excerpts from this text have previously appeared in the *Los Angeles Review of Books* and in *Intersubjectivity Vol. II: Scripting the Human*, eds. Lou Cantor and Katherine Rochester (Berlin: Sternberg Press, 2018).

CONTRIBUTORS

MASHINKA FIRUNTS HAKOPIAN is an Armenian writer, artist, and researcher born in Yerevan and residing in Glendale, CA. She is an Associate Professor in Technology and Social Justice at ArtCenter College of Design, and holds a PhD in the History of Art from the University of Pennsylvania. With Avi Alpert and Danny Snelson, she makes up one-third of the collective, Research Service. Her writing and commentary appear in *Performance Research Journal*, *Los Angeles Review of Books*, Meghan Markle's *Archetypes*, and elsewhere. Her research focuses on practices that generate alternative imaginaries of the future.

ANA IWATAKI is a writer, curator, and organizer from and based in Los Angeles. She is a PhD student in Comparative Studies in Literature and Culture at the University of Southern California. As a community organizer, she is embedded in a history of art and activism in Little Tokyo, Los Angeles.

ANURADHA VIKRAM is a writer, curator, and educator. Vikram's book *Decolonizing Culture* (Sming Sming Books, 2017) helped initiate a global movement to decolonize arts institutions and monuments. They have written for art periodicals and publications from Paper Monument, Heyday Press, Routledge, and Oxford University Press. They are an Editorial Board member at *X-TRA*, and faculty in the UCLA School of the Arts and Architecture.

FERNANDO DIAZ is a scientist whose work focuses on the quantitative evaluation and algorithmic design of information access systems, including search engines and recommender systems. His recent research concerns understanding the broader societal implications of artificial intelligence and related technology.

BECCA LOFCHIE is a designer, artist, and educator based in Los Angeles. This is her second book with X Artists' Books. You can see more of her work at beccalofchie.com.

The Institute for Other Intelligences
Published in October, 2022 by X Artists' Books, Los Angeles, CA.

This publication is part of X Artists' Books' X Topics (XT) series, a collection of single-author books, curated and edited by Anuradha Vikram and Ana Iwataki and focused on the writing and ideas of artists of color and other marginalized voices. XT engages timely topics affecting our world today—exploring the vital intersection of critical and imaginative possibility through the lens of the arts.

Edited by Ana Iwataki & Anuradha Vikram
Designed by Becca Lofchie
Illustrations by Fernando Diaz
Copyedited by Olivia Weber-Stenis
Printed by Bookmobile

Set in open source typefaces Authentic Sans, STIX Two text, and Noto Sans.

Library of Congress Cataloging-in-Publication Data is available on request.

ISBN 978-1-7378388-5-2

X Artists' Books
PO Box 3424
South Pasadena, CA 91031
USA
www.xartistsbooks.com